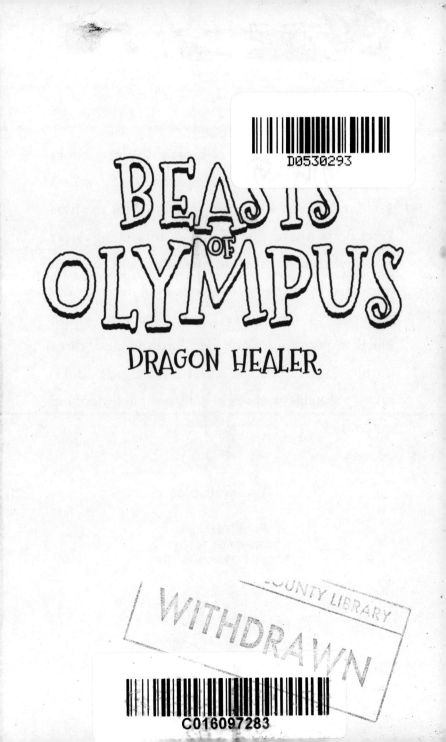

BEASTS OF OLYMPUS

DRAGON HEALER

Lucy Coats is the author of more than thirty books for readers of all ages, including *Atticus the Storyteller's 100 Greek Myths*, which was shortlisted for the Blue Peter Book Award. She began her storytelling career as a bookseller, editor and journalist, and has been fascinated by myths and legends ever since she can remember. She lives in deepest south Northamptonshire with her husband and three unruly dogs. When she is not writing, she cooks, grows vegetables and sits in her stone circle, looking at the stars.

Also available:

BEAST KEEPER
HOUND OF HADES
STEEDS OF THE GODS

BEASTS OF OLYMPUS

DRAGON HEALER

LUCY COATS

with illustrations by
David Roberts

Piccadilly
PRESS

First published in Great Britain in 2015
by Piccadilly Press
Northburgh House, 10 Northburgh Street, London EC1V 0AT
www.piccadillypress.co.uk

A CIP catalogue record for this book
is available from the British Library

ISBN: 978–1–84812–462–2
3 5 7 9 10 8 6 4 2

Typeset by Palimpsest Book Production Limited,
Falkirk, Stirlingshire

Printed in the UK by Clays Ltd, St Ives plc

Piccadilly Press is an imprint of the Bonnier Publishing Group
www.bonnierpublishing.com

For Debbie Hatfield, ace Arnie-wrangler
and most excellent editor,
and for David Roberts, whose fabulously beastly
illustrations make these books come alive.
With love and thanks, L.C.

1

RIOT IN THE STABLES

Demon, son of the beast-god Pan, and proud new bearer of King Poseidon's Order of the Ocean, shot up and out of the clear green waters of Melanie's spring.

'Urgh! Aggh! Pftth-aa!' he spluttered as his lungs adjusted to the warm, clean air of Olympus. Shaking his head to get the liquid out of his ears, he took a deep breath and let out a sigh of relief. The air smelled of fragrant flowers and honey, just as it was meant to. There was not a hint of stinky beast-poo, which meant that hopefully he wouldn't be turned into a pile of smoking Demon-shaped charcoal by a crowd of cross goddesses. Not today, anyway.

Melanie the naiad, who was sitting on a mossy rock, combing her long blue hair, gave him a nasty look as he struggled out, dripping, onto dry land, trailing his magic silver medicine box behind him. It was covered in great gouts and gobbets of slimy silver seaweed.

'Finished messing up my nice clean spring with that horrid salty sea stuff, have you?' she snarled angrily.

Demon picked a flapping flatfish or two out of his chiton and threw them back into the water.

'Yes,' he said, wondering why she sounded like a crazed chimera. Melanie was normally nice to him. 'I'm quite finished, actually. Er, is anything wrong? Only, you seem a little cross . . .' Melanie frowned and waved a hand towards the Stables of the Gods.

'Well, of course there's something wrong.

You've got to go and do something about those noisy beasts of yours, Demon. They've been bellowing and bawling ever since Hermes brought that nasty boy Autolycus up here. It's no wonder I'm cross. I haven't had a wink of sleep all week.' She yawned, showing two perfect rows of pearly white teeth. As his ears finally cleared with a pop, Demon heard a terrible racket coming from the Stables of the Gods. Now he knew exactly what Melanie meant. Without another word, he picked up his box and ran. What on Olympus was happening in there? It sounded as if every single beast was rioting and rumpussing out of control!

Inside the stables, it was complete chaos. Almost every pen had a baaing, neighing, screeching or shrieking beast leaping up and down. A tall dark-haired boy was whirling round and round in the middle of the centre aisle, laying about him with a brush and banging on the bars.

'Leave me alone!' he shouted. 'Shut UP, you horrid noisy creatures!' Demon dumped the medicine box on the floor, pulled out his father's magical pipes and blew a short, sharp blast. Immediately, there was silence.

'Who are YOU?' asked the boy, dropping his brush in mid bang. 'And how did you do that?'

'I'm Demon,' said Demon. 'Son of Pan and Official Beastkeeper to the Gods. And you must be Autolycus. What in the name of Hades' handkerchiefs have you done to my poor beasts to make them act like this?'

'Nothing,' said Autolycus sulkily. 'I've fed and cleaned the stupid creatures. What more do they want?'

'Huh!' said Arnie loudly to Demon, clacking its sharp beak against the bars of its pen. The griffin seemed particularly upset. '"*Nothing*" he says, the lousy, lying, thief! He's only gone and stolen half the wing feathers from the pegasi so they can't fly, AND he's hit Doris, AND he's tipped half the ambrosia cake down the poo chute!'

'Yes!' chorused the rest of the beasts. 'He did!'

4

'Hydra smacker!'

'Rotten robber!'

'Snackie stealer!'

'Feather pincher!'

'See?' said Autolycus. 'Garble garble garble! On they go, whimpering and whining. I don't know how you put up with it.'

'Stolen the pegasi feathers, eh?' said Demon grimly, stalking towards him as the noise levels rose again. 'Tipped the ambrosia cake down the poo chute? Hit my Hydra? HIT MY POOR HYDRA?'

A purple tide of rage was creeping up from Demon's toes. Nobody was allowed to treat his beasts like this! NOBODY!

Autolycus, seeing Demon's expression, looked worried. 'H-h-h-how? W-w-what do you mean? I-I-I never . . .'

'Oh yes you did,' said Demon, shouting to be heard over the racket. 'What you hear as garble, I hear as words, so don't try to deny it.'

'Oh all RIGHT, then!' said Autolycus sullenly.

'So what if I did? I only hit that idiot Hydra because it had dribbled all over the cake till it wasn't fit to eat, and it was only a few stupid feathers I took anyway, and . . .'

'And now poor Doris has bruises, and my winged horses CAN'T FLY!' roared Demon. Even though Autolycus was bigger than him, Demon suddenly felt he had the strength of ten stable boys. He grabbed Autolycus by the scruff of the neck and ran him out of the stables, past Melanie's spring and all the way over to the Iris Express.

'Stop it! Le' go of me! Get off!' bawled Autolycus. But Demon was determined to get rid of him.

'One passenger for earth, Iris!' he yelled, pulling handfuls of fluffy pegasi feathers out of Autolycus's chiton with his other hand as they went. 'And don't bother too much with the seatbelts!'

'HEY!' shouted Autolycus. 'Give those back! I could have sold those feathers for a FORTUNE! They're MINE!'

'Oh no they aren't!' said Demon, shoving him onto the see-through wisp of rainbow. 'I should hang on tight if I were you,' he added, as the Iris Express gave an eye-watering lurch and whooshed downwards. There was a sudden choked-off scream and some noisy retching, which trailed away into nothing. The Iris Express could be scary and sick-making if you had a weak stomach and no head for heights.

'Serves him right,' muttered Demon, picking up all the scattered pegasi feathers from the grass where they'd fallen and smoothing them out carefully. He trotted back to the stables, mumbling to himself and vowing never to go away again.

'Why can't the gods just leave me alone?' he grumbled as he walked into the comforting musty, dusty, beastly smell of the Stables of the Gods, the place he now called home. 'Every time one of them takes me away from my proper job it all goes horribly wrong up here. First it was Hades with poor old sneezing Cerberus, then

Poseidon with his itchy hippocamps.' Demon sighed a huge sigh. When would he ever get five minutes' peace?

The racket died down to a quiet rumble as he walked into the stables and went down the aisle, petting and stroking all his beasts and hearing their stories about how awful Autolycus had been to them. A big bubble of anger built up in his stomach again as he rubbed poor Doris the Hydra's bruises with arnica. How could people be so horrid to animals? He just didn't understand it.

'Oi! Pan's scrawny kid! Come over here and let me out,' came a snarky voice from the griffin's pen, breaking into his cross thoughts. 'I want a private word with you!'

Demon unlatched the griffin's pen and stalked out of the stables, Arnie padding behind on its huge lion's feet.

'What now?' he said. 'Spit it out. That wretched Autolycus left me a lot to do, in case you hadn't noticed.'

'Aaah!' sighed the griffin, stretching its wings in the bright sunlight and flapping them to get the dust out. 'That's better. I've missed being outside.' It gave Demon a sly look from one of its fierce orange eyes. 'Now, what was it I wanted to say? Ah, yes! I believe you owe me a little something, Pan's scrawny kid. A little something beginning with M and ending with T, with a tasty little E and A in the middle.'

Demon marched over to Arnie, standing on tiptoe until he was nose to sharp pointy beak with the great beast. 'No. I. Do. NOT!' he hissed. 'The deal was that you and the Nemean Lion had to look after the stables properly while I was away.' He gestured back through the doors at the mess of spoiled ambrosia, tipped-over poo barrows, wisps of golden celestial sun hay and fallen-over rakes – the stables looked as if a small hurricane had blown through. 'I don't call THAT properly!'

'It's not MY fault. Me and Lion were doing fine till Hermes brought that thieving oaf in,' said the griffin sulkily. 'I had the ambrosia cake locked away from Doris and everything. The whole place was spick and span and shining till Hermes came along and started meddling. That's when it all started to go wrong – that bratty boy Autolycus just didn't understand anything we said, and he didn't care about us either. Not like you do. Doris wasn't the only one he hit with that horrible brush, you know, but Hermes put an anti-beast protection spell round him, so we couldn't get him back.'

Demon sighed, all the anger draining out of him. 'I'm sorry he treated all of you so badly,' he said, stroking the griffin's rough lion pelt. 'I'm sure you did your best. I'll have a word with Hermes – see if he can't smuggle up a few juicy steaks from earth or something. Now, we'd better get back and start setting things to rights. As far as I can see it's going to take all day to get it sorted. But first I must see if my box has something to stick the feathers back on the pegasi. They said they were desperate to fly again.'

The griffin batted him with a paw, making him fall flat on his face. 'Good to have you back, Pan's scrawny kid. And I'll hold you to your promise about the juicy You Know Whats. If I don't get something decent to eat soon, even your skinny carcass is going to start to look tasty!' A long pink tongue swiped Demon's face. 'Yum yum!' it said, clacking its beak menacingly near his ear.

'Oh shut up, Arnie,' said Demon, scrambling to his feet and dusting his already filthy chiton down. 'You know I'd give you terrible indigestion. Now where's that box of mine?'

The silver medicine box was exactly where he'd left it: in the middle of the passage where he'd dropped it when he'd run into the stables. He picked it up and went down the row of pens till he came to the flying horses. Oh dear! They were a sorry sight. Their beautiful wings were half bald, their coats were dull, their tails were drooping and even the little golden horns in the middle of their foreheads looked sad.

'Itchy-scratch?' said Keith, the boss pegasus hopefully, presenting his left ear.

'Definitely,' said Demon. 'But first I need to get these feathers of yours fixed.'

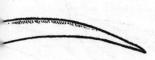

2
THE PYRO-PROTECTION KIT

Demon was just peeling bits of feather and icky-sticky stuff off his fingers after successfully mending the horses' wings, when the alarm from the carved head on the back wall of the stables started to squawk.

'Incoming! Incoming! Double-flaming incoming!' it yelled. 'Deploy Pyro-Protection Kit! Deploy Pyro-Protection Kit!' Demon had no idea what was happening. What did the head mean when it said 'double-flaming incoming'? And what was a Pyro-Protection Kit? He looked around frantically.

'Where do I get a Pyro-whatsit Kit?' he asked Arnie in a panicky voice. Demon didn't know what was coming but he'd been on Olympus long enough to know he needed to be prepared for whatever came through the stable doors.

'Hospital shed,' said the griffin. 'Third drawer on the left. Hurry up, Pan's scrawny kid. You haven't got much time before those things burn down the whole of Olympus. I'm off to fetch the Fire Officer.' Flapping its wings frantically, the griffin took off.

Demon didn't have time to ask what 'those things' were. Running faster than a speeding salamander, he raced over to the hospital shed, ripped open the third drawer on the left, and pulled out what looked like a floppy, silvery human body. It had a strange opening up the back, covered feet, and finger-shaped bits that he supposed were for his hands. Demon shook it out and turned it round and round. He guessed he was supposed to wear it. But if so, how did he get into it? He touched the small tag at the top of the opening. Was that a clue?

'Pull downwards on tag!' said a crackly voice. Demon jumped backwards in fright. 'Come on!' said the voice impatiently. 'Hurry up!' So Demon pulled, fumbling slightly in his haste. The tag slid down smoothly, revealing two sets of sharp teeth on either side.

'Climb in,' said the voice. 'And welcome to Hephaestus's Patent Pyro-Protection Suit. What is your fire situation level, please?'

'I don't know!' said Demon, hurriedly stepping into it, pulling the suit up over his body and slipping his hands through the sleeves. 'But I need to get to the Iris Express fast!' Immediately a hood flipped out and over his hair, and a clear mask sealed itself round his face as the tag shot upwards, fastening the two sets of teeth together behind his head with a crunch. Demon took a startled breath, but the air in the suit was cool and slightly scented with calming lavender.

'Pyro-Protection in place,' said the suit. 'You may now proceed safely to the danger zone. Please breathe normally.' Demon was already running again, as the rest of the silvery material moulded itself tightly to his body. There were loud, angry moos and bellows coming from the direction of the Iris Express, and there was an ominous cloud of smoke and sparks rising from above the rainbow.

As Demon skidded to a halt, he saw several things all at once. First, there were some trees on fire, their big bunches of silvery-golden fruit bursting with big squelchy pops in the heat. Then there was the grass, which had huge, steaming scorch marks across it. The main problem was obvious. Two enormous bulls with golden rings in their noses were roaring and rampaging about, snorting and spurting great gouts of fire out of their nostrils. Their hides had a strange metallic sheen, and everything they touched burst into flames. They were a little smaller than the Cretan Bull but looked twice as deadly. They had brass hooves which churned and pawed the ground, and their bodies were covered all over with deep cuts that ran with bright red streams of smoking blood. None of Heffy's inventions had ever let him down, so, trusting that the Pyro-Protection Suit would keep him safe, Demon darted forward through a wall of fire and grabbed the two bulls' nose rings. A gust of flame swept over him, but he felt it as no more than a warm bath of sunlight.

'Whoa!' he shouted. 'Calm down! I can fix your wounds, but you have to stop setting stuff on fire!' The two bulls took no notice. They both tossed their heads in the air at the same time, so that Demon lost his grip and went flying, just missing a sharp horn by a whisker. 'Oof!' he gasped as he landed flat on his back and rolled sideways into a patch of burning grass to dodge the flailing hooves. He reached for his pan pipes, but they were trapped inside the Pyro-Protection Suit.

'Get this thing off me! I need my pipes! Or a pocket?' he yelled, tearing helplessly at the shiny silver material. Immediately a bulge formed by his right hand.

'Pocket now operational,' said the suit.

As Demon grabbed the pipes and scrabbled them up to his mouth; the mask opened just enough for him to blow a short trill of notes. But, for the very first time, his dad's magical present failed him. The bulls just carried on rampaging. By now, fire was spreading everywhere, and shrieking nymphs were jumping out of trees and running from flower meadows, heading towards the shining white buildings where the gods and goddesses lived. Demon blew the pipes again and again in a hundred different ways to try and calm the frantic wounded beasts, but nothing worked. Just as he'd been tossed into the fires for about the twenty-fourth time, a thunderous shout came from behind him.

'Khalko! Kafto! Cease and desist, you fire-blasted bovines!' It was the blacksmith god, Hephaestus, Fire Officer of Olympus, with a crowd of automaton robots behind him. He walked through the flames, reached out two long, sooty arms and seized both bulls by the tips of their horns. Then he clashed their heads together and kicked their brass hooves out from underneath them, so that they crashed to the ground, the flames from their nostrils draining away to a dribble.

'Thanks, Heffy,' Demon groaned through his mask, rubbing his bruises as he got to his feet.

'No time for that,' said the smith god. 'Go and fetch a double dose of saffron crocus juice – the red kind, mind – and bring it back here as quick as you can while I put out these fires. It's the only thing that will save my bulls.'

Demon didn't argue. He limped back to the hospital shed as quickly as he could, grabbed the little glass bottle of red liquid from his stores, and limped back again. By the time he got there, Hephaestus had set five of his automaton robots to digging a big trench to make a fire break, and was flailing at the remaining flames with a bristly fire-broom in each hand. Khalko and Kafto were still lying on the ground, their terrible wounds smoking and bleeding onto the scorched earth, but their eyes were closed and their flames had died completely. Demon knelt down beside the bulls, his bruises forgotten. He hated to see any beast injured or unwell.

'Who did this to you?' he asked angrily. 'Was it that wretched "hero" Heracles again?' But the bulls didn't reply.

'Just treat their wounds with the saffron juice,' Hephaestus shouted as he batted out a spray of sparks. 'They'll be fine if you do that. I designed it specially for them!'

Wondering what the smith god meant, Demon smoothed a drop of the medicine onto every wound on the bulls' bodies, staining the fingertips of the Pyro-Protection Suit bright red. Hephaestus had to give him a hand with turning each of the huge beasts over, so he could do both sides. It took him a long time, but by the time he had finished, all the wounds had stopped smoking and were beginning to close up nicely.

'What happened?' Demon asked again, as the bulls opened their eyes and began to stir.

'Dragon men!' coughed Khalko.

'Jason!' coughed Kafto, letting out a small spurt of flame.

'I think I'd better get you both into a nice safe fireproof pen – there's one free beside the Cretan Bull,' Demon said. 'Then you can tell me all about it.'

'Off you go,' shouted Hephaestus. 'We'll finish up here. Good job, Pandemonius! Come and tell me how they are later.'

As Demon led the two bulls off towards the special pens at the back of the stables, he could hear Hephaestus chivvying some dryads into healing the trees and grass, and a gang of nymphs into dusting the soot off all the flowers. Soon Olympus would be back to its normal beautiful self.

'In you go,' he said, swinging open the big stone doors of the pen for the bulls to enter. 'Make yourselves comfortable. I'll just go and fetch you some nice silver hay to eat.'

'All sorted, Pan's scrawny kid?' asked Arnie the griffin, flapping down to meet him from its lookout perch on the roof. 'Everything under control? Any chance of you wearing normal clothes again any time soon? You look like a squeegee stick insect in that thing.'

Demon glanced down at himself. It was true. His legs did look rather long and spindly, encased in tight-fitting silver. But he wasn't complaining. The Pyro-Protection Suit had saved him from being frazzled to a crisp.

'You're just jealous you can't have one, Arnie,' he said, 'but I s'pose you're right. I'd better take it off now.' At once, the Pyro-Protection Suit's crackly voice sounded in his ear.

'Safety check. Please report on status of fire situation.'

'All clear,' said Demon. 'I'm well away from danger now.' Immediately, the suit began to loosen around him.

'Initiating undressing process,' it said as the hood and mask retracted. 'Pull tag in a downward direction and step out.'

It wasn't as easy as it sounded, because he had

to reach right round behind himself, but Demon eventually struggled out of the suit and bundled it untidily on top of a bale of sun hay outside the stables.

'I'll sort you out later,' he said.

'All folding assistance gratefully received,' said the suit. 'Thank you for your valued custom. Hephaestus's Patent Pyro-Protection Suit is here to serve all your flaming emergencies.'

3

THE BRASS BULLS

Once they'd munched some hay and settled down comfortably, the bulls told Demon their story.

'There was this hero, see?' said Khalko. Demon rolled his eyes. Heroes were mostly nothing but great big beast-battering bullies, as far as he was concerned.

'Yeah. Jason, he was called,' said Kafto. 'He beat us up and made us plough an enormous muddy field, and then he sowed all these teeth in it.'

'Dragons' teeth, he called them,' said Khalko.

'Only they didn't grow into dragons, they grew into dragon soldiers.'

'Stone ones, with axes and spears and swords,' said Kafto. 'They sprang up out of nowhere, and started fighting Jason.'

'And us,' said Khalko. 'Laying about them and stabbing anything that moved, they were. That's where we got all those nasty wounds.'

'What happened then?' asked Demon.

'Well, we don't really remember much after that, cos those dragon soldiers drove us a bit mad,' said Kafto. 'We sort of got a bit out of control, really. But I think I heard a girl yelling about putting something to sleep and telling Jason to hurry.'

'Yeah. And I saw Jason climbing up a tree that had a big furry gold bundle hanging on it,' said Khalko. 'Then we must have somehow got dead in the earthly realms and come up here.'

'Yes,' said Demon. 'That's what usually happens to you poor immortal beasts. And then I have to patch you up. Never mind, you'll be safe now. I'll bring you some more hay when you've finished that lot – you need building up after what you've been through.' There was a sudden bellow and a spray of sparks from the pen next door. Demon poked his head over the wall.

'All right, all right,' he said to the Cretan Bull next door. 'You can have some too. Greedy beast! Perhaps you can tell these two how horrible Heracles put out your fire while you're waiting.'

Demon hurried back with the cake and tipped it into the mangers. Soon the three bulls were mooing and munching together contentedly. Demon grabbed a broom and began to tidy up the mess that Autolycus had left. It took him all the rest of the day, and most of the evening, and by the time he'd eaten his own supper of fresh ambrosia cake, he was exhausted. He climbed the stairs to his little loft room above the stables, flopped down on the bed and pulled his spider-silk blanket over him, praying to Zeus that no more emergencies happened in the night. He had a bad feeling that he hadn't heard the last of Jason's misdoings.

Next morning, though, everything seemed as if it was back to normal. Demon trotted about the stables, barrowing poo, filling mangers, sweeping and chatting to the beasts.

'I missed you all,' he said to Doris, who was happily following him round, its nine mouths full of brooms and buckets. 'Poseidon's kingdom was interesting, and I'll miss having Eunice around. She's my new Nereid friend who likes hippocamps, you know. But I like being up here much better.'

'Snackies?' the huge green Hydra asked hopefully, dropping a bucket on his toes.

Demon hopped about. 'Later,' he said, rubbing his bruised foot. 'I'll have to go and ask the kitchen fauns to deliver some more supplies. Autolycus was right about one thing – you did drool on most of it.' He patted Doris's green flanks. 'Shame you didn't drown HIM in drool, really!'

After Demon had been to the kitchens, and

stacked the ambrosia cake neatly, he made his way to Hephaestus's workshop under the mountain. Loud bangs and crashes came from within, and he put his head cautiously inside, remembering the time when he'd made the mistake of entering when the forge was fired up in dragon mode. But the warning slate had no pictures of fearsome dragons or a skull-and-crossbones on it, so he went inside. Hephaestus was hammering away at an enormous silver and gold bowl, nearly big enough to take a bath in.

'What's that for?' asked Demon.

'Zeus wants it to give to some king he favours down on earth,' said Hephaestus, putting down his hammer and reaching for a smaller silver one. He began tapping away on the inside of the bowl, and under his clever fingers a picture of Zeus and his thunderbolts began to emerge on the outside. 'I'm putting a little magic in it, so that whatever food or drink is put inside will never run out. Now, how are those bulls of mine, young Pandemonius?'

'I meant to ask you about them,' Demon said. 'Why do you call them *your* bulls?'

'Yes, yes,' said the god testily. '*My* bulls. Khalko and Kafto. I made them, see? They're a bit like my automatons, made of brass with lots of gizmos inside. Gave them to the King of Colchis as a gift, years ago. Nasty piece of work, he is, but he did me a favour once.'

'Well, he didn't take very good care of them, did he, lending them to that horrible Jason person? I think they should stay up here now – I'll look after them much better than he did.' Then Demon frowned, remembering something. 'I s'pose that was why they didn't respond to my dad's pipes, if they're sort of robots – but then how come they were bleeding all over the place?'

'Ah! That's the ingenious part,' said Hephaestus, looking very pleased with himself. 'I wanted to make them as real as possible, so I invented a mixture that looked like blood to put inside them. That red saffron crocus juice is the main ingredient – which is why they needed it to heal them and replace what they'd lost.' He paused to wipe his brow with one grimy hand. 'By the way, young Pandemonius, I hope you've sorted out all that racket that was coming from the stables when you were off looking after Poseidon's fish-beasties. I meant to find out what was going on, but I've been busy. Which reminds me, you'd better get on out of here – I've got a big order of armour from Ares to do next, and that'll mean putting the forge in dragon mode.'

Demon didn't need telling twice. One encounter with the dragon forge was quite enough for anyone! As he trotted back to the stables, humming happily to himself, he heard a flap-flapping of wings above him.

'Oi! Pan's scrawny kid!' called Arnie, swooping down and landing in front of him with a puff of dust. 'You'd better get inside quick. There's some girl in there, and she wants to see you.'

'Does she have sort of aquamariney eyes and dark green hair?' he asked, beginning to run. Maybe it was his nereid friend Eunice, come to visit him from Poseidon's realm, he thought. Maybe she had a problem with the hippocamps again. He hoped it was her – he was really missing Eunice's company. He'd liked having a friend of his own age to talk to. The griffin snorted through its beak.

'Not exactly. You'll see. And I'd hurry if I were you. She doesn't look too happy.'

Demon saw all right, as soon as he skidded to a halt in front of her. The girl had long shiny black hair that coiled and moved by itself, bright snake-green eyes, and sharp pointy fingernails, which were clutching at her long white silk robes. She was older than Eunice, and she definitely wasn't a goddess, Demon knew that at once. She wasn't nearly scary enough. She wasn't a naiad or a dryad or a nymph either. The word that wormed its way into Demon's mind was . . . witch. She had a kind of dry, crackly, magicky smell about her.

'Er . . . what can I do for you, Ma'am?' he asked cautiously. It didn't hurt to be polite to someone who might have magic powers. You never knew what they might turn you into.

'Are you Pandemonius the beast keeper?' she asked. Demon nodded. 'Then you're the one I need,' she said, sounding relieved. 'Come with me.'

Demon's mind was racing as he followed her beckoning finger out of the back door of the stables and towards the poo chute, where the hundred-armed monsters roared and raged in Tartarus below. There was a light chariot parked beside the dung heap, with two small winged creatures yoked to it. They had long, sinuous bodies, spotted with black and gold, bright orange crests on their heads and tiny short legs with clawed feet. They were also lying down in their traces and panting with exhaustion.

'What in the name of Ares' armour are those?' Demon exclaimed.

'SHHH!' his companion hissed in a panicky voice, clutching his arm tightly with her sharp nails. 'Don't mention HIM! He might find me! I'm not supposed to be here at all!'

Demon wrenched his arm out of her grip. Witch or not, he wanted to know what was going on.

'I think you'd better tell me just exactly who you are, and why I should do you a favour,' he said sternly. 'I don't mind helping your beasts, but I'm not getting in trouble with the gods again – I've had quite enough of that, thank you very much!'

The witch girl immediately collapsed to her knees, sobbing. Demon felt terrible. He hadn't meant to make her cry.

'Come on,' he said, helping her up and taking her over to a nearby boulder. 'Sit down here.' He fumbled in his chiton and pulled out a grubby handkerchief, which he handed to her. She looked at it rather doubtfully before taking it and blowing her nose loudly.

'I-I'm P-Princess M-Medea,' she said. 'I'm in dreadful trouble with A-A- . . . er . . . the god of war for using my powers to help my boyfriend steal something from the god's sacred grove, and now he's threatened to k-kill me, so I have to go into hiding. O-only I can't take my flying dragons with me – everyone knows they're mine, so they'd give me away. My grandfather told me you were good with beasts, so I thought I'd bring them to you and see if you'd look after them. I was just going to leave them for you to find, but flying all the way up here has exhausted them, and now I'm worried they're going to d-die.'

As she began to sob again, Demon got up to look at the two small beasts. It had to be said the dragons didn't look too good.

'Wait here,' Demon said, wondering who the princess's grandfather was, and how he knew that Demon was good with beasts. 'I'll just go and fetch my medicine box.'

'Oh, do please hurry,' said Princess Medea. 'I'm not sure they can last much longer.'

4

A DAY FULL OF DRAGONS

Demon dumped the box beside the two dragons and tapped its lid politely. 'I need something to wake these poor beasts up, please, box,' he said, as Princess Medea hovered anxiously by his shoulder. 'I think they're just tired out, but could you have a look?'

The magic box began to glow blue and strange symbols ran over its silver sides. Two long tubes, each with a silver disc on the end, uncoiled and shot out from its top, clamping on to the dragons' chests. After a few seconds, they retracted with a snap.

'Extreme kourasitis detected,' said the box in its metallic warble. 'Remove remedy from medicine port and reboot subjects via mouth.' There was a small click and a bottle of bright orange liquid appeared, together with a silver spoon.

'What did all that mean?' asked Princess Medea. 'I didn't understand a word of it.' Demon sighed. As usual, the box was using its stupid cryptic language. Luckily he was used to it by now.

'Don't worry about it,' he said. 'I'm pretty sure it's just saying they're completely exhausted. The box always talks like that; I think Hephaestus designed it to be annoying on purpose. It does always come up with the right medicine in the end.' He poured out a large spoonful of the orange liquid and carefully dribbled it into the nearest dragon's mouth. It had a strange fringed top lip, which lifted up to reveal two rows of needle-sharp teeth. As he was finishing with the second dragon's dose, the first one opened its eyes, lunged sideways and bit his bottom. Hard. It burned like acid.

'Ouch!' he yelled, leaping backwards and clutching himself as Offy and Yukus, the two snakes who made up his magical healing necklace, raced down his back towards the wound.

'Bad dragon,' scolded Princess Medea. 'Don't bite the nice beast keeper. He's going to look after you while I'm away.' She looked at Demon. 'I must go before I'm caught up here by You Know Who,' she said. 'Take care of them, won't you?' Demon nodded as she took a vial out of her robe and tipped a drop on to her tongue.

'Ugh!' she said, as her body started to fade into a thin purple mist. 'Disgusting stuff. No wonder my Jason didn't like taking it.'

'Wait!' shouted Demon. What did Princess Medea have to do with the hero who'd hurt Hephaestus's brass bulls? 'What do you mean, *your* Jason?' But it was too late. Medea had disappeared in a puff of smoke.

The two dragons were writhing and thrashing

in their harness by now, and it took Demon a little while to get them calmed down and untangled. He had some questions for them about their mistress, but first he had to find out what kind of dragons they were, and find them a pen to live in.

'Are you fire-breathers?' he asked, wondering where it was best to put them, as they waddled towards the stables on their short stumpy legs.

'No, we're poison-spitters,' said one.

'And biters,' said the other, baring its teeth. 'Want me to show you again how well I bite?'

'Er, no thanks,' said Demon. 'I'm good. I'll put you next to the Giant Scorpion, then. Feel free to spit at him – he won't even notice.'

But just as Demon had settled his charges into their new home, the air in the stables darkened and became colder. A smell of unwashed bodies and old blood wafted into his nostrils, and he began to hear the sound of tramping feet.

'Oh no!' he whispered. Demon knew the sound of an approaching god when he heard it.

Two lines of fully armoured soldiers marched

into the stables, each with the sign of a bloody dagger on his breastplate.

'Halt! About turn! Present arms!' shouted one of them. With a metallic clatter, the soldiers turned to face each other, making an alleyway of crossed spears. Demon dropped to his knees and bowed his head as a gigantic figure in shining golden armour strode towards him. He didn't even have to lift his head to look. He knew exactly who had come to visit by the pair of gold-studded military-looking sandals that stopped right under his nose. It was Ares, God of War, accompanied by his godly bodyguards.

There was a rasp of metal, and Demon felt the tip of an unsheathed sword pressing under his chin to make him look up. He began to shake, but quickly stopped as he felt a sharp prick and then a bead of blood trickling down his neck. Ares gazed down at him with cold eyes the colour of a stormy sky.

'So, son of Pan,' said the god in an unexpectedly high voice, which had a faint air of battle and screaming behind it. 'We meet at last! I've heard so much about you. Quite the little healer, aren't you?' He lowered his sword and bent down, lifting Demon up by the front of his chiton and peering to inspect the small cut he'd made. 'Ah! Blood! How delightful. Nothing wrong with a little red blood, is there, boys?' He turned to look at his soldiers.

'Nossir! Nothing, sir!' shouted the godly bodyguards, beating their armoured fists against their chests. Ares waved a hand at them, and they snapped back to silent attention again. Demon felt a bit sick.

'You will come with me, stable boy,' said Ares. 'I have a beast of mine I wish you to attend to. Bring him.' Without another word, he flung Demon at one of the godly bodyguards and marched out. The guard caught him and set him down in the midst of them. They fell into formation behind their master.

'Hut! Hut! Hut! One two! One two! One two!' they yelled in unison, chivvying Demon along between them.

By the time he'd been marched through Olympus at what seemed like a million miles an hour, and been picked up again and thrown into the back of a war chariot with four plunging fiery horses harnessed to it, Demon was far too scared and winded to do anything other than lie there, every limb trembling. He could feel Offy and Yukus mending the cut Ares had made — his magical medicine box was back in the stables, so maybe they'd help him heal whatever beast it was that Ares wanted him to see to. If he survived that long. All he knew about Ares, from listening to the nymphs' gossip, was that he was the cruellest of all the gods, and that he worked with his sister, Eris, to sow hatred and enmity between the peoples down on earth. As the war chariot plunged downwards, Demon rattled and smashed against the sides, trying desperately to hang on to something . . . anything . . . with his fingernails. Ares' whip cracked and snapped over the horses' heads, as the god shouted and yelled for them to go faster.

'Pleasedon'tletmefalloutpleasedon'tletmefallout!' Demon muttered over and over again, keeping his eyes tightly shut as his fingers finally found a strap and clung to it for dear life. If they were going to crash to earth, he didn't want to see how far down it was. There was a loud thump and bump as the chariot wheels hit something hard, and Demon was jolted right off the back. He just had time to start to scream, when all the breath was suddenly knocked out of him as he dropped onto a bumpy surface, rolled once and came to a wheezing halt.

'You're late, brother,' said a peevish voice. 'And who's this piece of worthless junk you've brought with you?' A toe poked at Demon's heaving ribs, and he opened his eyes to see a hard-faced goddess looking down at him. Eris had short, black, greasy hair, a permanent sneer twisting her thin, bitten lips, and small, angry eyes. 'Is this what Zeus calls a stable boy? He looks more like a squashed beetle to me! And he smells like a dirty pigpen!' She turned away, disgusted, and stomped up a nearby hill, picking at a scab on her arm with one ragged nail.

'Stop lying there!' Ares screamed at Demon, waving his sword threateningly and jumping out of the chariot. 'There's work to do! Get up and attend to my wretched beast at once, or I'll chop your legs into mince and make you run round my parade ground for a century!' Demon scrambled up immediately, shaking with fear. Having his legs chopped into mince might just be an even worse punishment than being turned into a little heap of Demon-shaped charcoal. And it would certainly hurt more.

'Y-y-y-yes, Your M-m-m-military M-m-m-mightiness,' he whimpered. Ares strode off to join Eris and immediately started arguing loudly with her about who'd killed the most soldiers in the last war they'd started.

Demon looked around. Where was the beast? Finally he spotted it some way off, lying under a thicket of bushes in the middle of a grove of trees covered in golden leaves. Its huge flame-red serpentine body lay very still, with just a dying trickle of smoke coming from its jaws. Demon

began to run towards it. It was another dragon —
one about a hundred times bigger than Medea's
little poison-spitters!

Between him and the dragon was a muddy
ploughed field with what looked like grey rocks
lying all over it. As he got closer, though, Demon
saw that they weren't rocks at all. They were bits
of bodies. Stony arms and legs lay scattered around
like long grey boulders, with heads and torsos
piled up in heaps. He had to slow down to avoid
tripping over them. Some of the arms held spears
and swords in their hands. What kind of battle left
stone bodies behind? Then Demon saw a patch of
steaming red blood and a large bronze plough
tipped over on its side. Suddenly he remembered
the story Khalko and Kafto had told him.

'Jason!' he whispered. 'These must be all the
dragon-teeth soldiers he killed.' He started to run
again, leaping over the scattered stone limbs like a
deer. What if Jason had fatally wounded the dragon
too? What if Demon couldn't mend it? He thought
about Ares and minced legs, and ran even faster.

5

THE COLCHIAN DRAGON

The small trickle of smoke had almost evaporated when Demon finally reached the grove of golden trees. He flung himself underneath the thicket where the dragon lay and started to run his hands over its body, looking for wounds. Its rough, scaly hide felt pleasantly warm to the touch and he couldn't find anything wrong with it on the outside. He shook its shoulder, making its mane of spikes rattle.

'Wake up,' he begged. 'Oh please, wake up, dragon!' The dragon's eyelid twitched once.

'Go 'way!' it groaned, and its coils moved as it tried to pull itself into a tight ball. 'I'm not here. You can't see me!'

'Of course I can see you,' Demon said. 'You're right in front of me!'

'Am not,' it said. And it wrapped its tail around its head.

'What's wrong?' Demon asked. 'Ares sent me to help you, but I can't unless you tell me where it hurts.'

'Lalalalalalalalalala!' said the dragon, ignoring him and stuffing its claws in its ears. 'Lalalalalalalalalala!'

'Oh for Zeus's sake!' said Demon, exasperated. 'There's nothing the matter with you. I'm going to go back to the chariot and tell Ares you're fine. You're just in a stupid sulk about something.'

As Demon turned to go, suddenly a long red tail whipped out and trapped him within a tight coil of dragon. The coil began to squeeze.

'Am. Not. Sulking,' said a cross-sounding voice by his ear. Demon could hardly breathe, what with the squeezing and the hot, sulphurous fumes coming from the dragon's mouth. His ribs began to crack and pop.

'All right . . . all right,' Demon gasped with great difficulty. 'You're not sulking. I'm sorry. Just . . . just let me go . . . and tell me what IS wrong. I-I have to give Ares some sort of answer, or he . . . he'll . . . chop . . . my . . . legs . . . into . . . mince.' He was panting each word out one at a time now, almost unable to breathe.

The squeezing eased slightly. Demon felt something hot dripping on to his shoulder. Wriggling round in the coil that was still holding him, he managed to get a look at the dragon's head. Bright orange tears were streaming from its flame-like eyes, and, as they hit the air, they hardened into shining drops and fell to the ground with a tiny *plink*.

'Wow! What are *those*?' he asked, looking at the sparkling crystals. 'They're amazing! I bet all the goddesses would love to have you up on Olympus. They're always asking Hephaestus to make them new bracelets and stuff.' He got his hand free and stroked the dragon's long, thin horns. He decided to try a different tack with the sulking beast. 'Come on, I'm only Demon the stable boy. I'm your friend. You're safe with me. Tell me what happened to you.'

The dragon sighed, letting out another blast of sulphurous breath.

'Can't. Too ashamed,' it mumbled, letting go of Demon and wrapping its tail round its head again. 'Just kill me now and get it over with.'

Demon was outraged.

'Kill you?' he yelped. Then he clapped his hand over his mouth in case Ares heard. Lowering his voice, he went on, 'I've never killed a beast in my life, and I don't intend to start now. Anyway, you're immortal. You can't be killed. Why are you so ashamed? Did that nasty Jason do something awful to you?' But before the dragon could reply, there was a shout from across the stony battlefield.

'What's taking you so long, stable boy? Get that dragon up and running before I count down to one, otherwise it's minced legs for you – and maybe minced arms as well! *Ten . . . Nine . . . Eight . . .*

'Please, dragon,' Demon begged again. 'Just get up and come back to Olympus with me. We can sort everything out there, and I'll find you a lovely comfortable pen to stay in. If you don't, I-I-I'm g-going t-to b-be . . .' He was shaking so much he couldn't finish the sentence.

'*Seven . . . Six . . . Five . . .*'

'Oh, very well,' grumbled the dragon, uncurling itself, and beginning to slither over the stones towards the God of War, Demon running beside it. 'But I don't like it up there, you know. It's a hateful place. And the other beasts are always nasty to me!'

'*Four . . . Three . . . Two . . .*' A split second before Ares reached *One*, Demon and the dragon slid to a stop in front of him. Demon knelt immediately, thinking fast. He didn't know what was wrong with the beast, so he'd have to lie.

'I-I've examined your dragon, Your M-Martial M-Magnificence, a-a-and it . . . it's very sick. I-I think i-it may have been poisoned by Jason. I-i-it'll need a proper check-up in the stables, before I can make a f-final d-diagnosis,' Demon panted.

The dragon moaned loudly and coiled itself into a tight ball again.

'Sounds like you've got a great, big, fat case of cowardice here, Ares,' sneered Eris. 'That overgrown snake with legs doesn't look very poisoned to me.' She peered down at it malevolently. 'Does the poor ickle-wickle dragon need to run away up to Olympus for an ickle-wickle holiday, then?' she asked, in a horrid babyish voice. Then she turned to face her brother, hands on her skinny hips. 'I say stick it with your sword, and get rid of it! It's no use to you like this!'

Ares drew his sword and Demon tensed, ready to throw himself in front of the dragon. He couldn't allow it to be hurt, even if it meant being stabbed in the heart by the god himself. But instead of sticking the dragon, Ares whipped the sword sideways and in a trice he had it held to his sister's throat.

'No one calls the sacred Colchian Dragon a coward!' he snarled. 'And I wouldn't put it past that wretched whelp who Hera favours to have poisoned it, either. Jason had that witch-princess Medea's help, and she's famous for her vile brews!' He turned to glower down at Demon. 'I've got a nice little war in Aeolia I've got to go and stir up. Take this beast back to Olympus and have it fit and ready to report for duty by the time I get back, or . . .' He twitched his sword in a suggestive chopping motion towards Demon's legs, making them tremble with fear. 'Come on, Eris,' he yelled, jumping into his chariot. 'Time to shed a lake of blood!'

'Oh goody! What fun!' she squealed, leaping in beside him. 'I feel like a nice, noisy battle with lots of shrieking and screaming! Let's ask Alecto and her Furies if they want to join in too!' With a crack of the whip, the four fiery horses reared and raced up into the air.

What a horrible pair, thought Demon as the two deities disappeared out of sight. But he didn't say it out loud, just in case they were listening.

'Have they gone?' asked the dragon weakly, raising its head.

'Yes, thank all the gods, they have,' said Demon. 'And now I have to find a way of getting you back to Olympus.' He chewed on a thumbnail, thinking. Wounded beasts normally arrived at the stables via the Iris Express. But who called it for them down on Earth? He'd never thought to ask. If it was the god or goddess who looked after them, then he was in trouble. Ares had gone, and there were no other gods around.

'Can you call the Iris Express?' he asked the dragon hopefully.

'Oh no!' it moaned. 'I'm not summoning that thing. I'll fall through it. It's not safe.'

'That's what I thought when I first went on it,' said Demon soothingly, 'but it's fine, really. It's brought me all sorts of sick beasts, and never dropped one. Do you know how to call it? It would be a big help if you would.'

'If I really must,' the dragon sighed. 'But I warn you, you'll regret it if you take me up there.' Just then a long *paaaaarrrppp* sounded from its nether regions. The stench of rotten eggs and old socks almost knocked Demon over.

'Phew!' he said, fanning a hand in front of his face. 'We'll definitely have to find something to cure *that*! You're worse than the Cattle of the Sun on ambrosia!'

'I shall ignore that, as you have ignored my warning,' said the dragon huffily. Then it cleared its throat with a small explosion of red smoke. 'Iris Express for beast and boy! Olympus-bound!'

Nothing happened.

'Perhaps you need to say it a bit louder,' Demon suggested, breathing in shallowly through his mouth, and resisting the temptation to hold his nose. The smell was truly dreadful.

'IRIS EXPRESS FOR BEAST AND BOY! OLYMPUS-BOUND!' roared the dragon. As it did so, the sparks coming out of its mouth ignited the gas from its bottom with a loud *WHUMP!* Demon jumped back, beating out the small flames about to set light to his chiton. He could smell frizzling hair too, but just as he was going to reach his spare hand up to bat at it, a shower of rain sprinkled on him, soaking him to the skin. Shaking the water out of his eyes, and steaming slightly, he saw a blaze of rainbow light from the sky above.

'Celestial fire extinguisher activated,' said a familiar tinkly voice. 'Please ensure all flames are out before boarding.'

The Iris Express had arrived!

Demon was pretty sure he wasn't on fire any more, but he ran his hands over himself, just in case, before coaxing the dragon on board the wisp of nothingness.

'My dragon friend here is a very nervous traveller,' he said. 'Do you think you could provide your usual arrangement to tie us both on, please?' Immediately, rainbow-coloured ropes looped themselves around Demon and the dragon.

'Please hold on tightly for take-off,' said Iris, as she whooshed off into the heavens.

Paaaaarrrpppp! went the dragon's bottom again. Demon quickly sucked in a deep lungful of clean air before the pong hit. But he couldn't hold his breath forever. Choking and spluttering as the Iris Express landed, he was very relieved to stumble out into the fresh air of Olympus, with the dragon trailing reluctantly behind him.

6

STINKY OLYMPUS AGAIN

'Pooh!' said a passing nymph as they went by. 'What's that stink? You don't want the goddesses smelling *that*!'

'See!' muttered the dragon, his long thin horns beginning to droop. 'It's started already. They all hate me!'

'Don't be silly,' said Demon. 'Nobody hates you. And we'll have your . . . er . . . little problem fixed in no time. Just wait till I find my magic medicine box. It'll sort you out. Now come on, follow me. Let's get you into one of the special dragon pens.'

Demon trotted off in the direction of the stables, hoping that there would be no more *parping* on the way there. The nymph was right. If the goddesses got even one whiff of the dragon's stench near their laundry, they'd turn Demon into a pile of charcoal dust quicker than he could say stinky bum. The dragon heaved its heavy red coils behind him, leaving a trail of flattened grass behind it.

'Oi! Pan's scrawny kid!' hissed the griffin, stalking up behind him on its lion's feet. 'Where's that meat you promised me? I'm starving!' It clacked its beak hungrily near his ear.

'Not now, Arnie,' Demon said impatiently. 'Can't you see I'm busy? I told you I'd ask Hermes, and I will. But just at the moment . . . well . . . as you can see, we've got a new beast in the stables, and I've got to take care of it right away.'

'Huh!' said the griffin, lashing its tail. 'Colin the Colchian Dragon, isn't it? I remember you. Didn't old Soldier Sandals drag you off to one of his sacred groves to guard something? What was it now? I forget.'

'The Golden Fleece,' muttered Colin, looking behind itself shiftily. 'And don't call my boss that – he's got ears everywhere, you know.'

Sneering in its usual manner, Arnie turned round, flapped its wings once, and flew off to its perch on the roof. Demon led the dragon towards the very back of the stables, pulled open the heavy flame-proof doors and took it into the deepest cave of all. He crossed his fingers and hoped that the thick rock would keep any smells from leaking out.

'You have a nice lie down and close your eyes, Colin,' he said. 'I'll go and fetch my box and then you can have something to eat.' But just as Demon was about to walk away Colin looped him with its tail again, preventing him from leaving.

'Please don't go!' it said.

'Why not?' Demon asked. 'Don't you want me to try and make you better?'

'Yes,' said Colin. Its voice sounded sad, so

65

Demon stroked its horns gently. 'B-But I need to tell someone what happened down there, or I'll burst!' As if to back up its words, it let a tiny *paaarp* out of its bottom. Demon buried his nose in its warm scales, trying not very successfully to block out the resulting stink as the dragon began its tale.

'I guarded the Grove of the Golden Fleece in Colchis for years, never sleeping, always on watch. They called me Old Observant Eyes, and I was proud of the trust Ares had placed in me, his very own sacred dragon. I even gave up my teeth willingly to his friend King Aeetes, because I knew that they would grow strong soldiers to help me defend my master's grove.'

'Oh!' said Demon, interrupting. 'So they were *your* teeth Jason sowed in that field?'

'Yes, yes,' said the dragon, a little testily. 'I'm getting to that bit. Now don't interrupt again, or I shall squeeze you.' Demon shut his mouth quickly. His ribs still ached from the last squeezing Colin had given him.

'I had one friend in the world,' the dragon went

on. 'Or I thought I did. Medea the witch-princess, King Aeetes' daughter, used to come and visit me every day. She was the one who harvested my teeth once a year, and she did it so gently that I never even felt them go. She used to polish my scales with a soft cloth and sing to me. Then, last week, a ship arrived on the shores of Colchis. A ship full of heroes. I knew they had come to steal the Golden Fleece, because Medea told me so. She said that their leader, Jason, was very cunning, and asked me to keep specially alert, to watch as I'd never watched before. She said that she would bring me some of her special juniper potion to put on my eyelids so that I would be able to see in all directions.' Colin's voice sounded thoroughly miserable now.

'It was a trick. I allowed her to paint the potion on my eyelids and I waited for it to work. But instead of being able to see in all directions, my eyes closed and I fell into a trance – I, the unsleeping, ever-wakeful Colchian Dragon failed my master!' Colin's eyes began to water. 'I saw

Jason in my dreams as Medea smeared him with an ointment of invincibility,' it went on. 'I saw how he mastered Khalko and Kafto. I saw him plant my teeth, and fight the stone warriors who rose up from the ground. I felt him climb over my sleeping body and cut down the Golden Fleece with his sword. I saw him run to his ship, with Medea laughing beside him as she made both of them invisible to her father and his soldiers.'

By now, the hot tears were running from the dragon's eyes, and fire jewels were plinking and pinging all over the rocky floor of the cave. 'I-I was so ashamed to have f-failed that I wanted to disappear,' it sobbed. 'I s-still do! I don't d-deserve any k-kindness, and besides, I-I've been banished from Olympus. Ares must have forgotten that when he t-told you to bring me up here. Last time, the goddesses said that they'd send me down to Tartarus to live with the hundred-armed monsters if I ever came here again, b-because I'm s-such a s-smelly beast.' It let out another tiny *parp* and the cave filled with more of its noxious stink.

'S-see!' Colin wailed. 'This is what happens when I get upset! No one can cure me! Just leave me alone! I *deserve* to go to Tartarus!' It unlooped its tail from around Demon's body and coiled itself into a hiccuping dragon ball of misery.

Demon didn't know what to do. He wanted to comfort the poor beast, but he was about to choke from trying not to breathe.

'I'll be back soon with my box,' he said. 'Try not to worry – I'm sure we'll be able to find a cure somehow. And I won't let anyone send you to Tartarus.'

As soon as he got back into the main stables there was a tremendous clamour.

'Food!' bellowed the three fiery bulls.

'Food!' whinnied the pegasi.

'Food!' roared the Nemean Lion.

BANG! went the Giant Scorpion's sting against its pen door.

'Snackies,' drooled Doris the Hydra, clattering its brooms and buckets.

'All right! All right!' yelled Demon. 'I'm

coming!' He fed his charges as quickly as he could, and went to fetch the box from the hospital shed. Running his eyes over the shelves of medicinal herbs and plants, he spotted a bunch of peppermint leaves and a bottle of oil. Peppermint was good for the digestion – maybe that would help to settle the dragon's stomach.

'Come on, box,' he said, picking it up by its silver handles. 'We've got a patient to examine.' But the box lay silent in his arms. He gave it a shake. 'Hey! Wake up,' he said. 'We've got work to do.' The box gave a small shudder, flashed blue and opened its lid a fraction. Then, with no warning, thousands of tiny, brightly coloured bugs poured out of it, covering the box in a seething mass of feelers and tickly legs, which started to crawl up Demon's arms.

'Ugh!' he said, dropping the box hurriedly, and trying to brush them off. They fell to the floor and vanished in a twinkle of tiny sparks. 'What is the matter with you? What are those things?'

A muffled metallic voice came from underneath

the mass of bugs. 'Debug required. Debug required. Exiting all programs. System crash imminent.' With that, it snapped shut and went still and silent once more.

Demon stamped his foot angrily.

'WHY?' he shouted, running his hands through his curly hair till it stood on end. 'WHY DO YOU ALWAYS GO WRONG JUST WHEN I REALLY NEED YOU?' He kicked the box so hard that it fell on to its side.

'Dear me, Pandemonius,' said a voice from the doorway. 'I'm not sure Hephaestus would be very pleased to see you treating his gift like that! Is there a problem?' Demon looked up and saw a tall, thin god with a mischievous smile on his face.

'Yes!' he said grumpily. 'There is. I've got a depressed dragon with stinky stomach gas, and now my stupid medicine box has decided not to work, so I can't find out what's wrong with the beast. If the goddesses smell the stink, I'm charcoal, and Colin the poor Colchian Dragon will be sent to Tartarus. And if I don't cure it, Ares will mince my legs and arms up and make me run round his parade ground forever!' He sat down on the box with a thud and dropped his head into his hands. 'I might as well ask Hera and the rest of them to sizzle me now. Then at least it would all be over.'

Hermes, chief messenger of the gods, laughed. 'Come on,' he said, pulling Demon up. 'Let's take your box to Hephaestus. He'll be able to mend it in no time. He did make it, after all.'

'But what if he can't?' asked Demon.

'Then we'll think of another plan,' said the god. '"Never despair", that's my motto. There's always a solution if you look in the right place!'

7

HEPHAESTUS AND HERMES

Demon trailed along behind Hermes, his heart somewhere underneath his sandals. Despite the god's cheerful words, he knew he didn't have much time. Colin's disgusting smell was much worse than the problem he'd had with the Cattle of the Sun when he'd first arrived on Olympus. And if its stinky stomach gas built up too much in the rocky pen, there was a risk of the whole stables exploding – maybe even the whole of

Olympus itself. Demon tried not to imagine what Zeus would say about that! Zapped by a thousand lightning bolts would be the least of it. Suddenly he skidded to an unexpected halt, as a beak seized the back of his chiton with an ominous tearing sound.

'Oi! Pan's scrawny kid!' hissed the griffin, spitting out bits of cotton. 'Have you asked him yet?' Demon closed his eyes and breathed hard. This was so NOT what he needed right now. But he *had* promised. And although the griffin was often friendly, he knew he'd better not test its patience.

'Hermes!' he called to the god, who was now some way ahead, leaping up the path to Hephaestus's mountain as if he were a goat, and singing a rude little rhyme about a nymph and a shepherd. 'Could you come here a minute, please?' The god turned and made his way back down the path.

'Ah, my old friend Arnie. And how are you on this fine sunny day? Bitten anyone good lately?'

Demon cleared his throat.

'Er, he thinks you owe him some nice big juicy steaks, Your Goddishness,' he said. 'After the Autolycus thing.'

Hermes frowned. 'What Autolycus thing? What's the little scamp been up to now?' He peered around. 'That reminds me. Where is he? I thought he was supposed to be helping out?'

'Well, I-I kind of threw him down the Iris Express,' said Demon, a bit nervously. Hermes was a friendly god, and he'd always been kind to Demon – but, as Demon had learned to his cost, gods could change from nice to nasty in the blink of a griffin's eye. 'He . . . he was stealing pegasi feathers, a-and hitting all my beasts with a broom. And he left the stables in a horrible mess, too!'

'Oh dear,' said Hermes, luckily not seeming at all cross. 'Well, he was the best I could do at short notice. I did warn you he's not very trustworthy. Did you get the feathers back?' Demon nodded. 'Well, I'll have a stern word with him anyway when I see him next.' The god looked at the griffin, puzzled. 'Why do I owe you steak, though?'

'Me and the Nemean Lion were doing a good job of looking after the stables till your boy came along,' muttered Arnie. 'Demon promised us meat if we did it properly, but then Autolycus messed it all up for us. So I reckon you owe us at least a year's worth of steak.' It looked at him in a calculating way, its orange eyes sly and cunning, and clacked its beak hungrily.

'Hmmn!' Hermes said, narrowing his sky-blue eyes and tapping one finger against his staff twirled with golden snakes. 'A year's worth of steak, eh? Are you sure you and that lion were doing such a good job? Don't I remember seeing a Giant Scorpion heading towards Zeus's palace? Didn't I have to help you get it back in its pen?'

'Thatwasjustamistake,' Arnie mumbled, looking a bit embarrassed.

Demon's mouth fell open. The Giant Scorpion had escaped? And no one had thought he ought to know about that?

'You can have a day's worth of steaks when the gods next have a feast,' Hermes told him. 'And that's your lot. Now, be off back to the stables with you, cheeky beastling. Pandemonius and I have work to do.'

'I'm sorry he bothered you,' said Demon apologetically as the griffin flew off with a clatter of golden wings. 'I didn't know about the Giant Scorpion.'

'Don't worry about it,' said Hermes. 'I don't mind getting him a steak or two to keep him happy. We all get fed up with ambrosia sometimes, though don't tell Hestia I said so.'

The sun was setting in a blaze of red just behind Hephaestus's mountain as they arrived, and a trickle of black smoke was drifting from its peak. Inside the forge, there was a clattering and clanging as six of the smith god's automaton robots loaded trolleys with shields, breastplates, bits of armour, swords and spears.

'Ho! Brother Heffy! Where are you?' Hermes

yelled over all the clamour. Hephaestus emerged from behind a trolley, wiping his grimy forehead with a stained spotty handkerchief.

'Here!' he boomed. 'Hang on a minute. I've just got to get this lot off to the Iris Express. Ares needs them for some war he's waging down in Aeolia.'

Demon gave a small sigh of relief as the trolleys rattled out of the cave mouth. If Ares was still off fighting his stupid war, he wasn't going to be coming to find out if his dragon was cured or not.

'What's the problem NOW?' asked the blacksmith god as the last trolley left and the forge quietened to a low hum of crackling flame and bubbling metal. Demon held out the silver medicine box.

'I think it's broken,' he said. 'There were all these insect things crawling out of it, and then it went dead.'

'That doesn't sound good. Did it say anything?' asked Hephaestus. Demon repeated the strange words as best he could.

'Well, that's ALL I need,' said the god grouchily. 'A system debug. It means taking the whole box apart with tweezers and making sure the bugs haven't bred in the programs. I'm very busy right now – Zeus wants to give Hera a new necklace to wear to a wedding, and he insists I should use a jewel none of the other goddesses have.' He scratched his head. 'I can't fix that box for at least a week, maybe more.'

Demon felt as if he'd been punched in the gut. He'd never keep the dragon gas under control for a whole week. He let out a huge groan as Hermes bent towards him.

'Leave it to me,' Hermes whispered in Demon's ear, then he stepped forward and slung an arm round Hephaestus's broad shoulders.

'Can't you do it any sooner, Heffy? Zeus may be a bit cross if he doesn't get Hera's necklace, but if the other goddesses smell what Demon's hiding in the stables, then I don't like to think what will happen. Remember how they treated little Eros when he set off a stink bomb at one of the feasts

– and he's a god? It would be much worse for Pandemonius!'

Hephaestus shuddered. 'Yes. I do remember. Poor Eros – he had to go into hiding for weeks till his feathers grew back.' Hephaestus sighed. 'What wretched beast have you rescued now, Pandemonius?' he asked, looking at Demon in a resigned kind of way.

As Demon explained about Colin the stinky Colchian Dragon and its gas problem, Hermes seemed to be looking at something caught in Demon's sandal straps.

'Hold still a minute!' said the god. Bending down, he wiggled the sparkly thing loose and held it up to the light, making red and orange shimmers and glimmers dance over the cave walls.

'What in Zeus's name is that?' asked Hephaestus eagerly. He pulled the jewel out of Hermes's fingers and turned it round and round, examining it closely.

'Oh,' Demon said. 'It's just something the stinky dragon makes when it cries. There are loads of them all over the floor of its pen. Sort of fire jewels, I suppose.'

'I'll make you a deal,' said Hephaestus, seizing a piece of charcoal and starting to draw jewellery ideas on a slate with a manic gleam in his eyes. 'If you bring me every one of that beastie's tears, I'll get the box back to you as soon as ever I can. These fire jewels are just perfect for Hera's new necklace. I've never seen the like! Can you keep the dragon penned in that back cave for a bit?'

'Well, I suppose so,' said Demon doubtfully. 'But – '

'That's the spirit,' Hephaestus said. 'Off you go now, Pandemonius.' He clapped him on the back, then turned to fiddle with something on a nearby shelf, his clever fingers working fast. He handed Demon a dusty black face mask. 'And take this! It should help.' Then he shooed Demon and Hermes out of the cave, and started shouting for his automatons to bring him gold and silver.

'There,' said Hermes, as they made their way

back down the mountain. 'I told you there was always a solution!'

As he barrowed a load of ambrosia cake mixed with peppermint leaves into the dragon's new home, Demon wasn't so sure. He was now wearing the charcoal-filled mask that Hephaestus had given him so that he could breathe, but even so the smell still just about knocked him over. He closed the doors quickly behind him.

'Hello, Colin,' he said as cheerfully as he could through the mask. 'I've brought you something to eat. It's got nice soothing herbs in it for your tummy.' The dragon was still curled up in a red ball of misery, so Demon tipped the ambrosia cake out beside it.

'What herbs?' it asked, raising its head. 'If it's peppermint, don't bother. Doesn't work. I quite like it, though.' It uncurled itself and sniffed at the ambrosia cake, flickering out a long forked tongue to taste it. Then it sighed mournfully. 'I just *knew* it would be peppermint. Oh well, I suppose it's better than nothing. And at least my breath will smell better. Where's that magic box of yours, then?'

'Um, I'm afraid it's not working. Hephaestus is mending it as fast as he can. Do you think you can manage not to . . . er . . . I mean . . .' He gestured delicately at the dragon's tail, hoping it would understand. 'Just until I have the box back again.'

'I'll try,' said the dragon, through a mouthful of ambrosia cake. 'But it's really hard to keep it in.'

'And please can you keep the sparks in too?' Demon asked. 'Only I don't want the whole stables to explode.'

The Colchian Dragon eyed him crossly. 'All right, all right! You've made your point. No sparks, no gas. I'm not stupid, you know.' It went back to munching ambrosia cake and peppermint, dribbling saliva over the floor. It was almost as messy an eater as Doris.

Once Demon had swept up all the fire jewels and delivered them to Hephaestus, he put the rest of the beasts to bed. Climbing up to his loft, he sniffed carefully. No stinky gas smell yet. He crossed his fingers hopefully as he pulled the spider-silk blanket over him and went to sleep. Maybe he'd get away with it after all.

8

AN ERUPTION OF GODDESSES

Demon was woken by the sound of choking and spluttering from the beasts below.

'Stinky dragon! Stinky dragon!' they all shouted in their various beastly voices. Demon's nose was suddenly assaulted by a terrible smell.

Pulling his chiton straight and leaping out of bed, Demon raced down the stairs and through the stables, grabbing his mask as he went. As he opened the doors the gas in Colin's pen rushed out in a great gushing wave, and he heard a thump behind him as one of the smallest pegasi fainted.

'What happened?' he tried to ask. But the dragon-gas stink was so bad he had to turn tail and run, slamming the doors behind him. Some of the beasts in the stables were wheezing and choking horribly, and Demon knew he had to get the worst affected ones out immediately. But where could he put them?

'Think, Demon, think!' he said to himself, trying to wipe his streaming eyes with both hands. Then he remembered the paddocks at the back of the stables, where the winged horses sometimes grazed. 'Come on!' he croaked, unlocking pens as fast as he could. 'Follow me! And please try not to eat each other!' Finally he had all the beasts out, except for the Giant Scorpion, which didn't seem to be affected so he left it where it was. He led the beasts to the paddocks and let them in, and then ran back for the pegasus who had fainted. Lugging and tugging its heavy body into a cleanish poo barrow, he wheeled it away as fast as he could, its four limp legs hanging over the edge and its floppy black wings dragging over the ground.

The scene that met his eyes in the paddock was one of absolute chaos. The Nemean Lion was growling ferociously as it stalked one of the Cattle of the Sun, Medea's poisonous dragons were in a spitting fight with the Caucasian Eagle, and the unicorns were kicking the winged horses. Demon wrenched his dad's pipes out of his chiton, ripped off his mask and blew the knock-out emergency series of long trills his dad had taught him after the feast when he'd been made Official Beastkeeper to the Gods. Immediately every beast lay down and fell into a deep and unbreakable sleep – all except for Khalko and Kafto, the two Bronze Bulls, who were immune to his pipes, being half automaton.

'Can I trust you two to behave, and not breathe any sparks?' he gasped. The smell was less strong out here, but still bad enough to make his head reel.

'We'll be good,' they said. 'This nice green grass is a treat after all that dry hay.'

Just as Demon was going back to the stables to try and tackle Colin again, he spotted what looked like a multicoloured whirlwind of dust coming towards him. Before Demon knew what was happening, it had picked him up and whisked him away.

'Put me down!' he yelled, batting at it uselessly. But the whirlwind only held him tighter. Within seconds it had tipped him out on to a smooth, cold surface. Demon scrambled to his feet, sick, spluttering and furious. And then he saw three pairs of icy goddess eyes glaring at him across a sea of white marble. All the rage drained out of him in a whoosh, and utter panic took its place. Was the thing he had feared most about to happen? Was he about to be turned into a Demon-sized heap of charcoal? He tried to scrabble backwards, but all his limbs seemed frozen.

'WHAT IS THAT DREADFUL STINK?'

shouted three furious goddess voices. The combined sound was like a swarm of boiling mad bees, like a hundred packs of howling hounds, like a thousand berserk bears. It caught Demon in a great tornado of noise and flung him backwards across the slippery floor, stealing all the breath from him. He landed in a limp heap by a large pillar, unable to move or think.

A long and dreadful silence fell, as the three goddesses waited for him to reply. Choking and coughing, Demon fought for air, his eyes closed. Somewhere inside him, a little voice was screaming for help. He knew he was doomed to be that heap of charcoal within seconds if he didn't answer!

'Oh, by the Echidna's eyeballs,' said a voice behind him. 'What are you all doing, terrifying Zeus's poor wretched stable boy like that? Here, lad. Drink this!' Demon felt a cup pressed to his lips and he gulped thirstily, opening his eyes to see Hestia, Goddess of the Hearth, standing beside him, a large silver ladle in her other hand.

'What's this all about?' she asked, quite unafraid of the nasty looks her fellow goddesses were sending her from across the room.

'Have you no sense of smell, Hestia?' asked Eos, Goddess of the Dawn. 'My best bedsheets stink to high heaven!'

'My poor dear hounds' noses will never be the same again,' said Artemis, Goddess of the Hunt, patting the heads of two hairy, red-eared dogs which sat at her feet.

'My prettiest pink silk nightdresses reek of cesspits,' said Aphrodite, Goddess of Love.

'AND IT'S COMING FROM THE STABLES!' yelled the goddesses together, as they pointed at Demon, with three fire-spitting fingers. Hestia fended off a flurry of jagged sparks with her ladle.

'I-I-I'm s-s-s-s-s-sorry, O-o G-G-Goddessy G-Gloriousnesses,' Demon stammered. 'I-I-I'm t-t-trying t-to f-fix it as f-fast as I c-can.'

'And just what is this "it"?' asked Eos in a dangerously quiet voice. Demon closed his eyes tight and braced himself. There was no way he could avoid telling them.

'The-the-the C-C-Colchian D-D-Dragon's s-stomach g-gas,' he whispered.

'COLIN THE COLCHIAN DRAGON?' Artemis shouted angrily. 'But we banished that revolting beast from Olympus years ago! Why have you brought it back?' Demon cowered as she reached for her silver bow in one swift movement, and nocked an arrow to the string. Artemis never missed a shot.

'Now now, Artemis dear, put the bow away. I'm sure there's a sensible explanation,' said Hestia soothingly.

'There'd better be,' growled the huntress. But she lowered the arrow so it was pointing at the ground.

'A-A-Ares commanded me to bring it to the s-s-stables and cure it, Your A-A-Amazing A-Accurateness,' Demon told her. 'A-and th-then it a-all w-went a b-bit wrong.'

Artemis frowned, but next door to her

Aphrodite let out a tinkling laugh. The sound was like a waterfall of warm honey, smooth and sweet and delicious.

'A bit wrong?' she giggled. 'The whole of Olympus smells like a mixture of sulphurous sewers, unwashed ancient socks and rotten eggs, and you call it "a bit wrong"'?' She leaned back and fanned herself with a bunch of pink ostrich feathers as Demon blushed.

'W-well,' he said cautiously. 'M-maybe a whole lot wrong, would be a b-better w-way of p-putting it, Y-your B-Beauteous B-Bountifulness.'

Eos sighed. 'I suppose if that numskull idiot Ares commanded you, it's not really your fault,' she said. 'All he ever thinks about are his wretched wars. But what are you going to do about it, Pandemonius? None of us can go outside, the nymphs have all had to have a lie down, the flowers are wilting, the dryads have fled down to earth and the naiads have all disappeared underwater.'

'Ah! I wondered why no one but the fauns came

into the kitchen for breakfast this morning,' said Hestia. 'If the Colchian Dragon's here again, that would explain it. The kitchen crew and I haven't been able to smell anything since our chilli powder experiment exploded yesterday morning, so we haven't noticed anything.' She looked down at Demon. 'Why haven't you used that box of yours on the beast, though? I thought it was supposed to cure everything.'

'It is, Your Celestial Chefness,' said Demon glumly. 'But it's broken and Hephaestus can't mend it till he's made a necklace for Zeus to give Her Royal Majesty.' He looked around nervously, hoping the Queen of the Gods wouldn't pop out suddenly from behind a pillar. If Eos, Artemis and Aphrodite were scary, Hera was just plain bone-crumblingly terrifying.

'You're lucky, Pandemonius,' Aphrodite said, winking at him. 'Heavenly Hera's not on Olympus. She and Zeus are having a little private holiday together to make up after their last argument. They won't be back for a few days.' She leaned over towards the other goddesses. 'The Io episode, you know!' she hissed behind her hand.

'Just as well for you, stable boy,' said Artemis, slinging her bow again, and sliding the silver arrow into her quiver. 'But if you don't find a cure for that smelly dragon quickly, you'll find I can be just as fierce as Hera – and believe me, I'll set my hounds to tear you apart if you fail. I'm off down to earth to wrestle a few wolves – at least it doesn't stink in the woods. Come on, girls!' She whistled to her dogs and strode out of the room.

'I must go too,' said Eos. 'It's time I fed my poor Tithonus. He likes a grain or two of corn for his breakfast, and he'll only take them from my hand.' She shook a finger at Demon. 'Cure that beast of his disgusting problem, stable boy, or I'll hang you up by the ears on my washing line for a year.'

Aphrodite waited till the dawn goddess had gone, and then she sniggered. 'Poor Eos! Imagine having a grasshopper for a husband. That'll teach her to ask Zeus for a favour when he's in a bad temper!' She glided over and took Demon's hand. Close up, she smelled of roses and lily of the valley, with a hint of orange blossom. Demon breathed in deeply, and then felt his head spin and his knees grow weak. It wasn't wise to get too close to the Goddess of Love, even if the nice smell did mask the stink of dragon a bit.

'Come on, Pandemonius,' she purred in her silky voice. 'We'll go and see if that grimy husband of mine can't be persuaded to hurry up with fixing your medicine box. I'll take you to his forge by my secret underground passage. That way we can avoid going outside.' Then she gave him a sleepy sideways smile and another wink. 'You can tell me all about that pretty nereid Eunice on the way.'

Demon blushed. How did Aphrodite know about Eunice?

'Don't be so nosy, Affy,' Hestia said, pointing her silver ladle at the other goddess. 'You know boys don't like talking about all that lovey-dovey stuff!' She ruffled Demon's curls. 'Come and see me in the kitchens soon, Pandemonius. I'll be making a new batch of those honey cakes you tested out for me. Zeus and Dionysus can't get enough of them!'

9

THE CENTAUR HEALER

As she dragged Demon through rocky passages deep underneath Olympus, Aphrodite kept up a steady stream of gossip and inquisitive chat, asking him a whole load of snoopy questions about Eunice and the other nereid girls he'd met down in Poseidon's watery realm. By the time they entered Hephaestus's apartments at the back of the forge, Demon was redder than an overripe cherry.

'Oh, Heffy, darling!' cooed the goddess down a silver tube that hung coiled up by the door.

'Where are you? Your lovely Affy wants to talk to you!' Within a few minutes there was a sound of harrumphing and stamping, and Hephaestus came in dripping with water, and trying to wipe both his face and his hands clean at the same time. Seeing Demon, he stopped dead.

'What are you doing here, Pandemonius?' he asked, frowning. 'How did you get into my private rooms?' Aphrodite glided forward and laid a soft, white hand on his arm.

'Don't frown, Heffy, dearest,' she said. 'It makes you all wrinkly. I brought him. You know how I hate nasty stinky stinks, and that horrid dragon belonging to Ares is making all our lives a misery. Pandemonius really does need that magic box to cure it. You're so clever, I know you can mend it in a trice, and then everything can go back to smelling normal again.' She threw herself at Hephaestus and covered his beard with kisses.

Demon's face was now verging on purple with embarrassment. Hephaestus himself was spluttering and looking most uncomfortable as Aphrodite wormed her way under his arm and looked up at him expectantly through her long eyelashes.

'The thing is, my dear,' he said, harrumphing loudly, 'you know I'd do anything for you, but the damage to the box is worse than I thought. The bugs have eaten away all the workings inside, and there's one magical part in there that it took me weeks to make. I'll be as quick as I can, but I can't promise anything. Pandemonius will just have to try and find another way to cure the dragon's stenchy stomach.' He glanced over at Demon. 'Have you tried peppermint?'

Demon nodded. 'It doesn't work,' he said.

Aphrodite stamped one tiny foot and burst into tears. If possible, she looked even more beautiful when she was crying.

'I can't bear it,' she said, wriggling out from under Hephaestus's arm again. 'I won't have it!' She stamped her foot again, and a flock of cross-looking turtle doves erupted from the floor and flew round Demon and Hephaestus's heads, pecking them and beating them with their wings. 'FIX IT!'

she shouted, pointing a finger at Demon as she flounced out. 'Or I'll turn you into a myrrh tree and chop you down to make arrows for Eros!'

'Oh dear,' said Hephaestus, fending off beaks and claws. 'She will too, Demon. You'd better cure that dragon, or you'll end up as kindling.'

'But I don't know how!' Demon wailed. 'And the smell's so bad I can't get near it, even with your mask!'

'I think,' said Hephaestus, scratching his grimy beard thoughtfully, so that flakes of charcoal and ash fell onto his leather apron, 'that it's time to call in the heavy cavalry. We need Chiron the centaur. I'll send you down to Mount Pelion to get him.' The smith god looked serious. 'Chiron's your only hope. He's Zeus's brother, and a god in his own right, but the two of them don't get on too well sometimes. He'll take some persuading to come up here – and I don't know if even he can sort this mess out!'

Hephaestus flung open the door to the forge. 'Come on, we need to hurry! I still have to finish off that necklace for Zeus!' and off he strode. 'Keep the fires low,' he roared at the automaton robots as he marched past them. 'And keep the fans going. We don't want any of that dragon gas building up in here! I'll be back in a minute.' Reaching out to his workbench, he snagged two masks and tossed one at Demon. 'Put that on! It's better than the prototype I gave you yesterday.'

Then Hephaestus took a deep breath, clapped his own mask over his beard, and left the forge at a run, Demon at his heels.

'IRIS!' he bellowed. 'URGENT DELIVERY FOR MOUNT PELION!' The rainbow whooshed into sight immediately. 'Take Pandemonius to Chiron's cave, quick as you like,' he said. With that, the smith god turned on his heel, and raced back to his forge. 'Good luck,' he yelled over his shoulder.

The Iris Express dumped Demon on the very top of a mountain. It had groves of silvery wild olives growing on its steep flanks, and in the distance, Demon could see the blue-purple shimmer of the sea. As Iris's rainbow faded back into the sky, a huge creature trotted out of a nearby cave. He had a bright chestnut horse's body, but his bearded face and hairy torso were that of a man. He smelled of sweet herbs and wild places, and he had kind deep blue eyes that Demon felt could look right inside him. This had to be Chiron.

'Please, Your High Healeryness,' he said, dropping to his knees at the centaur god's front hooves. 'You've got to help me.'

'Whoa! Whoa!' said Chiron, holding up a green-stained hand. 'Who are you, young man? And how did you get the Iris Express to deliver you here? You're not a new god, are you?'

'Hephaestus sent me,' said Demon. 'I'm Pandemonius, son of Pan, but most people call me Demon a-and I've-got-a-sick-dragon-with-stinky-stomach-gas-and-the-goddesses-are-going-to-hunt-me-down-and-hang-me-up-and-turn-me-into-a-tree-if-I-don't-cure-it-and-anyway-the-gas-is-going

108

-to-blow-up-Olympus-a-and-Ares-is-going-to-mince-my-legs-a-and . . .' he ran out of words and came to a stop, gasping for breath.

'Well, you do seem to have a problem, don't you?' said Chiron gravely, his bushy eyebrows twitching. 'I think you'd better come into my cave and tell me exactly what's going on.'

Inside Chiron's cave was the most amazing healing space Demon could ever have imagined. It made his own hospital shed look like a joke. Shafts of natural sunlight from windows set high in the mountainside lit up shelves and shelves of neatly arranged bottles and jars filled with powdered herbs, roots, and many-coloured pills and potions. Hanging from the stone roof were drying racks with muslin bags full of leaves, blossoms and berries. There was a sparklingly clean operating table with gleaming rows of instruments, and a canvas hoist set to one side of it. There was a bench with pestles, mortars and knives for chopping, and, behind a curtain, he could see another cave room with rows of neatly made empty beds piled with folded blue blankets. There were also piles upon piles of open books scattered about with drawings of different sorts of human and beast anatomy, as well as the parts of plants and flowers. Demon stared around him in amazement.

'Here,' said the centaur, stirring a bright red powder into what looked like purple grape juice. 'Drink this. It'll give you energy and strength. I can see just from looking at you that you're carrying a heavy burden around.'

Between sips of the drink, which was delectably cool and tongue-tinglingly sharp, Demon retold his story. As he did so, he could feel a delicious sense of well-being spreading over his whole body. 'Hephaestus said you're my last hope,' he finished.

'I see,' said Chiron. One front hoof pawed the ground, and his large green-stained fingers tapped out a thoughtful rhythm on the scrubbed wooden bench. 'So you want me to come up to Olympus to try and cure this beast, do you, Demon?' Demon nodded, crossing his own fingers behind his back. He badly needed some luck here.

'But what about my pupils? What about my own patients? They need me too. I can't just leave them with no healer,' the centaur said. 'And I hate Olympus. Wretched place. All those gods and goddesses throwing their weight around – especially my thundery brother. I like the peace and quiet I get down here on earth.'

'Oh please,' Demon begged. 'I'm sure it won't take long. And Zeus is away at the moment, so you won't have to see him. Don't you have anyone down here you can leave in charge?' He peered past Chiron's smooth brown shoulder into the cave with its empty beds. 'You don't seem to have any patients right now.'

'Well . . .' The centaur god paused. 'I suppose there's nothing immediately urgent in the way of patients. I sent the last one home to convalesce this morning – that silly boy Melanion got savaged by a bear. And I suppose Asclepius could keep an eye on things and teach the apprentices. I've only got two at the moment – young Kokytos and his friend Actaeon.' He looked at Demon sternly. 'But I'm only coming up to Olympus for a short while, mind. Just until I've solved the dragon's stomach problem. I'm pretty sure I know what will cure it, but we'd better take several of my potions, just to be sure. Wait here while I go and make the arrangements.' Calling for Asclepius, Chiron cantered out of the cave and away through the olive groves.

Demon occupied himself by leafing through the books. He couldn't understand the funny squiggles underneath the pictures, but the drawings were amazing, and soon he was completely absorbed, his finger tracing the whorls and curlicues of the inside of a snake's ear, and then the way a set of bean seeds fitted exactly inside their furry pod. There was just so much he didn't know!

When Chiron came back a short while later, he grabbed a green gauze bag and handed it to Demon, who was almost dancing with relief that the centaur had agreed to help him. 'Watch and learn, young Demon,' he said, picking out a whole array of bottles, ointments and powders and putting them in the bag Demon was holding. Stretching up for a bunch of bright-blue berries with one hand, he grabbed protective leather goggles, surgical masks and wintergreen-soaked nose plugs with the other. 'If you're going to do the job properly, you can't always rely on that magical contraption of Hephaestus's to come up with the answers. You need to learn how to cure those beasts in the stables by yourself.'

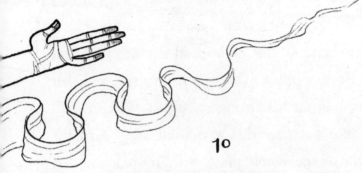

10

THE APPRENTICE HEALER

Armed with the eye goggles, thick surgical masks and nose plugs, Demon and Chiron climbed aboard the Iris Express. It was just as well they were prepared, because when they arrived on Olympus a dreadful, greenish haze was floating over the whole place, and it looked completely deserted. Clearly everyone was huddling inside the palaces with the windows sealed tight, trying to keep away from the smell. The flowers were drooping, and the trees were shedding leaves at a dreadful rate. Even the wintergreen-soaked nose plugs didn't keep out the stench entirely.

'Iris,' said Chiron in a muffled voice. 'Go and fetch Boreas, please. Tell him it's urgent, and that he must bring his strongest bag of winds. We'll need him to blow this gas cloud away into the heavens or the whole place will go up at the first spark.' Demon had never seen the Iris Express leave so fast. Clearly the rainbow messenger didn't want to linger anywhere near Olympus either, and he didn't blame her.

'Take me to your dragon,' said Chiron. 'And get on my back, it'll be faster.' Chiron knelt so that Demon could climb on so he rather gingerly clambered onto his broad horse's back. It felt odd and rather irreverent to be riding a god! With a lurch, the centaur got to his hooves and took off at a straight gallop, glass bottles clinking dangerously against each other in the green bag. Demon clung on with his legs and flung his arms round Chiron's muscly waist. He just had time to think that riding a centaur was quite different to riding Keith the pegasus, and then they were hurtling past the Giant Scorpion and pulling up at the dragon pen.

'Carefully does it,' said Chiron, opening the doors a crack. A thick cloud of deep green fog billowed out as they entered, too thick to see through, so they retreated outside again. 'It's no good,' the centaur said. 'We need to wait for Boreas to blow it all away. Let's stay outside. He shouldn't be long.' Demon said nothing. He couldn't. He was too busy trying not to faint, taking tiny shallow breaths through his mask and worrying about Colin. No wonder the poor beast was in a worse state than ever, what with people slamming doors on him and running away all the time.

Suddenly Demon shivered, ducking as a spatter of large hailstones fell out of the sky, stinging his bare arms and shoulders with their coldness.

'Here he comes,' said Chiron, pointing upwards. Suddenly the green haze scattered, and against the clear blue sky, Demon saw a stallion made of wispy white clouds, and on its back a purple-winged god with curly snow-white hair and a white beard stiff with frost.

'Ho! Chiron! What can I do for you? Iris said it was urgent,' said the God of the North Wind, leaping off the cloud horse. He fanned a purple wing in front of his face. 'Faugh! What a stink! No wonder you're wearing those mask things.'

'Yes, it's terrible, isn't it?' said Chiron. 'Young Demon here has a dragon with a badly upset stomach. We need you to unleash your winds and blow the gas away quickly so that we can get to it and begin treatment.'

The wind god laughed.

'No sooner said than done,' he said. 'Two strings will do it, I think. Hold on to your hats, boys!' Unhitching a stout leather bag as round as a bubble from his belt, he unfastened two of the strings at its neck, one red, one black. Immediately two enormous gusts of wind burst out. Each had a merry face, with puffed-out cheeks.

'Command us, O Master of Storms!' they said.

'Blow my winds, blow!' cried Boreas. 'Take

every trace of this stinky beast's stench and scatter it to the heavens!'

The winds obeyed, blasting themselves all over Olympus in a trice, entering every nook and cranny where the gas lurked, whisking stray straws, fallen leaves, dust, grass, hair, feathers, petals and one of Aphrodite's pink silk nighties up, up, up into the clean air above. Gathering all the gas into a whirling green cone, they sucked it high into the sky, right over Hephaestus's mountain. Suddenly, as one stray spark drifted up from the rocky chimney and hit the cone, there was a huge bang, and a flash of green and violet flame. Everything in Olympus rocked on its foundations, and then the gas was all gone.

'Thank you, Boreas,' cried Chiron, ripping off his mask and goggles, and blowing out his nose plugs as the wind god waved farewell and galloped off into the heavens. 'Now, quickly, Demon. We must get to the dragon before it has a chance to start up again.' Demon ran to the dragon pen doors and flung them wide.

Colin was sprawled on the floor of the back pen in a mass of quivering red serpentine coils. Its flame-like eyes were revolving in its head, and it was repeating *mustholditin-mustholditin-mustholditin* in a high, scared mumble as it shivered and shook in a kind of petrified trance.

'Right,' said Chiron, entering with a clatter of hooves. 'Get these down it immediately. Three ladlefuls of each.' He handed Demon three bottles, one orange, one yellow, one a virulent bright green, and a small golden ladle.

Carefully setting the bottles on the floor, Demon awkwardly wedged the dragon's jaws open with one arm, risking a bite from the long sharp teeth. 'One. Two. Three,' he counted over and over again, as nine ladlefuls of medicine slid down its gullet. He and Chiron waited anxiously as long minutes ticked by and there was no response from the beast. It continued to shiver, shake and mutter intermittently.

'Never mind,' said Chiron, holding out the large, sticky, strong-smelling ball of blue goop that he'd been mashing between his hands while they waited. 'Let's give it one of these. It's my patent stomach gas remedy for stubborn cases. If this doesn't work, then nothing will. Stuff it right down as far as it will go. Here, I'll hold those jaws apart for you.'

The centaur went down on his front legs, then folded his horse haunches underneath him, reaching out with sticky hands to draw the dragon's jaws wide open. Demon took the squishy, slippery mass and pushed it deep inside the dragon's throat till his arm had disappeared up to the shoulder. Suddenly, the dragon swallowed, and Demon felt his fingers begin to burn as a sudden spray of sparks popped upwards.

'Ouch!' he yelled, whipping his scorched arm out and shaking it frantically. Colin began to cough out gobbets of pale purple-blue fire, sending more sparks whizzing around the cave.

'Here,' said Chiron absent-mindedly, his eyes fixed on the beast, which was now gulping and gargling ominously as if it was going to be sick.

Reaching into the green bag and pulling out a pot of pale blue ointment he waved it in Demon's direction. 'Dip your fingers in this.'

Just as a blissful coolness was washing over Demon's burnt bits, the dragon gave a loud belch, which smelled strongly of ginger. 'That's it, old chap,' said the centaur, stroking Colin's long, thin horns. 'Let it all out. You'll soon be right as rain.'

Three enormous burps later, Chiron let out a big sigh of relief. 'That's what I wanted to hear,' he said. 'You should be fine now.' Turning to Demon he said, 'I'll show you how to mix up my remedy before I leave. If you give a dose four times a day for the next month, the dragon should be cured. But it must stay on Olympus till the course of medicine is finished, and you'll have to keep it warm and make sure its mind is occupied so it doesn't fall into an anxious state again. I can see from the state of its scales that it's been eating completely the wrong diet. It shouldn't be a red dragon at all – its natural colour is purple. It needs to eat plenty of charcoal, and have regular doses of fennel seeds and ginger on its ambrosia cake.'

The Colchian Dragon was looking perkier by the minute. Its eyes had stopped revolving now. It shook out its coils, and rattled its spines.

'By Ares' spear!' it said, nosing along its own body. 'I haven't felt this hungry since I was a dragonling. Did someone mention charcoal? I could quite fancy a nice big bowl of charcoal to crunch.'

'You can come with me and fetch some from Hephaestus's forge as soon as I've got the other animals back in their pens,' said Demon, patting the dragon. 'I'm so glad you're feeling better.'

Chiron stayed with the dragon while Demon went out to the pasture. The beasts lay scattered about the field where he'd left them, all still fast asleep. Khalko and Kafto were grazing contentedly among them. He fumbled in his chiton for his pipes, and put them to his lips. Blowing a soft whisper of sound into each beast's ear, he woke them one by one and led them back to their pen in the stables.

By the time he came to the griffin, who he'd left till last, he was exhausted. The sun was high in the sky, and he'd had nothing to eat that day, and nothing to drink since Chiron's potion.

'Hello, Pan's scrawny kid,' said Arnie, stretching and yawning. 'Cured that stinky thing, have you? Where's my steak?'

Demon laughed. Things were definitely back to normal!

An hour or so later, when everything in the stables was back in order, and he was leading the way up the steep path towards Hephaestus's forge, the Colchian Dragon slithering behind him, Demon suddenly had a brilliant idea.

'Are you there, Heffy?' he called. 'I've brought you a visitor.'

Hephaestus appeared in the door of the forge, looking dishevelled.

'We're not exactly prepared for visitors, young Pandemonius,' he said. 'Those winds Boreas let out may have blown all the stink away, but they've also knocked over all the stuff in the forge and blown the fire out. The robots and I have got a terrible mess to clear up; there's ruined charcoal crumbs all over the place, and I don't know how we're ever going to get the Zeus-blasted forge going again, so I can finish off that necklace for Hera.'

Demon beamed at him. This was going to be much easier than he'd thought. His brilliant idea might just work. 'Meet Colin the Colchian Dragon,' he said, gesturing behind him. 'The answer to all your problems!'

'Ah! So this is the beastie that's caused all the trouble, is it? Cured now, are you?'

'Yes,' said the dragon. 'And I'm STARVING!' It snapped its jaws hungrily. Hephaestus backed away from the sharp teeth hastily, then he frowned.

'Well, I don't know what you want me to do about it,' he said. 'I'm not a dragon restaurant. And what do you mean — it's the answer to all my problems?'

'Well, that's the clever bit,' said Demon, feeling

smug. 'The Colchian Dragon needs a new job to keep his spirits up – at least till Ares comes back from his war. He loves charcoal, so he can eat up all the ruined stuff for you – it won't matter to him if it's a bit crumbly – and he can easily light your forge and keep it going. Chiron tells me that once he's properly better his fire is the hottest of any dragon's. Meanwhile, he needs somewhere warm to curl up while he's convalescing. You can have a real dragon on hand when the forge needs to be put in dragon mode!'

Hephaestus scratched his head. 'You seem to have it all worked out,' he said. 'And how do you feel about it, dragon?'

But Colin didn't answer. It had slipped past Hephaestus and was busy gobbling down charcoal as fast as it could crunch.

'I think it likes it here,' said Demon. 'I'll be back with its medicine later. It's a very nice dragon now it doesn't smell any more!'

'You're a scamp, young Demon,' grumbled Hephaestus, stepping over the dragon's coils to go back into the forge. The tip of the dragon's arrow-shaped tail was already turning a bright royal purple. 'But I suppose you've got a good heart.'

Demon met Chiron back at the stables, where the centaur god had checked out all the beasts to make sure they hadn't come to any harm from being asleep for so long. Then he and the centaur went over to the hospital shed.

'Not bad,' said Chiron, looking around approvingly. 'Clean, neat and tidy. That's what I like to see.' Demon blushed as Chiron continued. 'I saw you looking at all those books I've got in my hospital. I've a good mind to ask that thundery brother of mine to let you come down to Mount Pelion once a week so I can teach you the basics of good healing. Would you like that?'

'Oh yes, please! I WOULD!' said Demon, a big grin exploding on to his face. He hadn't actually known it till this exact minute, but having a proper healing teacher was just what he really wanted.

'I've got so much to learn, though, especially

if you think I ought to be able to manage without the box,' he said. 'I've never had to heal any beast without it before.'

Chiron reached into his green gauze bag and started pulling out ingredients.

'Then let's start your lessons right here, young Apprentice Healer,' he said. 'No time like the present.'

Demon sighed happily. Apprentice Healer. He liked the sound of that title VERY much!

GLOSSARY

BEASTS:

Basilisk *(BASS-uh-lisk)*: King of the serpents. Every bit of him is pointy, poisonous, or perilous.

Bronze Bulls: Fire-breathing bovines Khalko and Kafto, who were created by Hephaestus for King Aeetes of Colchis.

Celestial Horses *(SELL-ess-tee-ul)*: Giant stallions who pull Helios's chariot and the sun from east to west every day around the Earth.

Cerberus *(SER-ber-us)*: Huge three-headed, snake-maned hound, Guardian of the Underworld, and Hades' favourite cuddly pet.

Colchian Dragon *(COL-chee-un)*: Ares' smelly pet and guardian of the Golden Fleece. Watch out for sparks if he farts . . . BOOOOM!

Cretan Bull *(KREE-tun)*: A furious, fire-breathing bull. Don't stand too close.

Griffin *(GRIH-fin)*: Couldn't decide if it was better to be a lion or an eagle, so decided to be both.

Hippocamps *(HIPPO-camps)*: Part horse, part fish. A sort of sea-horse, if you like.

Hydra *(HY-druh)*: Nine-headed water monster. Hera somehow finds this loveable.

Ladon *(LAY-dun)*: A many-headed dragon that never sleeps (maybe the heads take turns?)

Medean Dragons: Two poison-spitting, biting beasts that pull the witch-princess Medea's chariot.

Minotaur *(MIN-uh-tor)*: A monster-man with the head of a bull. Likes eating people.

Nemean Lion *(NEE-mee-un)*: A giant, indestructible lion. Swords and arrows bounce off his fur.

Pegasi *(PEG-a-sigh)*: Mini flying horses with cute gold horns.

Stymphalian Birds *(stim-FAY-lee-un)*: Man-eating birds with metal feathers, metal beaks and toxic dung.

Telchines *(TELL-keens)*: Underwater monsters with dog heads and seal flippers. Scary.

GODS AND GODDESSES:

Amphitrite *(AM-fih-TRY-tee)*: Sea Goddess and Poseidon's wife.

Aphrodite *(AF-ruh-DY-tee)*: Goddess of Love and Beauty and all things pink and fluffy.

Ares *(AIR-eez)*: God of War. Loves any excuse to pick a fight.

Athena *(a-THEE-na)*: Goddess of Wisdom and defender of pesky, troublesome heroes.

Artemis *(AR-te-miss)*: Goddess of the Hunt. Can't decide if she wants to protect animals or kill them.

Boreas *(BOH-ree-as)*: Icy God of the North Wind. Carries a handy bag of bouncy breezes.

Chiron *(KY-ron)*: Centaur God – part horse, part man – brother of Zeus and humungously awesome healer of all ills.

Dionysus *(DY-uh-NY-suss)*: God of Wine. Turns even sensible gods into silly goons.

Eos *(EE-oss)*: Goddess of the Dawn. Married to Tithonus, a grasshopper.

Eris *(AIR-iss)*: Goddess of Discontent. Argumentative, likes war and blood just a bit too much.

Hades *(HAY-deez)*: Zeus's youngest brother and the gloomy Ruler of the Underworld.

Helios *(HEE-lee-us)*: The bright, shiny and blinding God of the Sun.

Hephaestus *(Hih-FESS-tuss)*: God of Blacksmithing, Metal, Fire, Volcanoes, and everything awesome.

Hera *(HEER-a)*: Zeus's scary wife. Drives a chariot pulled by screechy peacocks.

Hermes *(HER-meez)*: Mischievious Messenger God with a handy invisibility hat and winged sandals.

Hestia *(HESS-tee-ah)*: Goddess of the Hearth and Home. Bakes the most heavenly treats.

Iris *(EYE-riss)*: Goddess of the Rainbow and messenger of the gods. Also a slightly sick-making form of transport between Olympus and Earth. Seatbelts, please!

Persephone *(per-SEF-oh-nee)*: Goddess of Spring, stolen away by Hades to be his wife. Made bad mistake of eating pomegranate seeds in the Underworld.

Poseidon *(puh-SY-dun)*: God of the Sea and controller of supernatural events.

Zeus *(ZOOSS)*: King of the Gods. Fond of smiting people with lightning bolts.

OTHER MYTHICAL BEINGS:

Arachne *(ar-AKK-nee)*: Brilliant weaver. Turned into a spider by Athena for boasting about her skill. Oops.

Ascelpius (ass-KLEEP-ee-us): Healer apprentice to Chiron and the first ever doctor. Burnt to a crisp by daddy Zeus.

Autolycus *(AW-toe-lie-CUSS)*: A very naughty boy. Stole some cattle and blamed it on Heracles.

Cherubs *(CHAIR-ubs)*: Small flying babies. Mostly cute.

Dryads *(DRY-ads)*: Tree spirits. Only slightly more serious than nymphs.

Epimetheus *(ep-ee-MEE-thee-us)*: Prometheus's silly brother who designed animals. Thank him for giving us the platypus and naked mole rat.

Eurydice *(YOUR-id-ee-see)*: Tree-nymph and all-time greatest love of Orpheus. Stepped on a snake by mistake. Died.

Geryon *(JAYR-ee-un)*: A cattle-loving Giant with a two-headed dog.

Heracles *(HAIR-a-kleez)*: The half-god 'hero' who was given twelve impossible tasks by scary Hera, including stealing poor Cerberus from the Underworld and dragging him up to Earth. Loooves killing magical beasts.

Jason *(JAY-sun)*: Fleece-stealing hero, basher of bulls and captain of the good ship *Argo*.

Lethe *(LEE-thee)*: Memory-stealing spirit of forgetfulness. Lives in a marsh.

Medea *(Med-EE-ah)*: Tricksy witch-princess, dragon-owner and girlfriend of Jason.

Maenads *(MAY-nads)*: Followers of Dionysus, lovers of dancing and partying.

Naiads *(NYE-ads)*: Water spirits. Keeping Olympus clean and refreshed since 500 BC.

GRIFFIN

Description: Head and wings of an eagle, body of a lion. This beast is as tall as a donkey, with a tawny golden coat. It is quite lazy, and likes to sleep with its eyes open. When pleased, it will purr loudly, but when angry it has a deafening screech that can cause small earthquakes. If you're lucky enough to gain its grudging respect, you can call it Arnie. Artemis demands all Arnie's old wing feathers for her arrows, since griffin feathers are known to fly true and straight. It is impossible to lie in front of a griffin.

Favourite Foods: Raw lamb with a sprinkling of scarab beetles and blood gravy.

Likes: Perching on roofs, being a know-it-all, scaring heroes, sandy deserts, sarcasm.

Dislikes: Heracles, being threatened, smelly cows.

Dangers: Beware of toxic spit, which can cause horrible burns. Beware also lightning-fast beak and claws. Griffins are good at escaping, so make sure of your stable security.

Demon's Top Tip: Always be polite. Do NOT annoy or threaten a griffin. Misunderstandings are usually fatal to humans.

HYDRA

Description: Much misunderstood gigantic green nine-headed water-monster with a rough, scaly hide, which lives in a swamp when on Earth. Has short, stumpy legs and a long, serpent-like body. It may look fierce, but is as gentle as a puppy if treated kindly. It belongs to Hera, scary queen of Olympus, and isn't the most intelligent beast in the Stables, though that may be because of Horrible Heracles chopping all its heads off. It now answers to the name Doris, and is very good at carrying extra buckets and brooms. A beast of very few words, it has a loud purr and is very affectionate.

horse on Olympus is called Keith. They are very acrobatic fliers and love to do tricks in the air. Once a year they team up with the cherubs and fire spirits to give the gods an aerial flying display.

Favourite Foods: Ambrosia cake and clotted cream, silver lyre grass (only found in the Olympian fields).

Likes: Looping the loop, showing off, being groomed, brushed and oiled.

Dislikes: Dragons, mice.

Dangers: Will kick and bite if annoyed, otherwise fairly safe.

Demon's Top Tip: If you want to ride one of the flying horses, find out where their 'itchy bits' are. They can usually be bribed to let you on their backs by a good long scratching session.

GIANT SCORPION

Description: Just like a 'mortal' scorpion, only about a hundred times the size. Belongs to Apollo, who sent it to sting Orion the Hunter in the heel. Has armour-plating as thick as a tank and a two-foot-long sting.

Favourite Foods: Eats stardust and eggs of giant spiders when it can get them.

Likes: Does not like anybody or anything, really, but enjoys stabbing its sting into other beasts and snapping its pincers at them while they dangle.

Dislikes: Everybody and everything.

Dangers: Sting mostly fatal except to other immortal beasts. Pincers strong enough to crush skulls.

Demon's Top Tip: Do NOT go near this beast except when strictly necessary. Take a long stick to fend it off. Be ready to run. Keep door firmly locked with at least two magic padlocks at all times.

DEMON'S GUIDE TO BEASTCARE

CAUCASIAN EAGLE

Description: A gigantic bronze-coloured eagle belonging to Zeus, and one of his official messengers. It has the daily job of tearing out the liver of the Titan Prometheus, who stole fire from the gods. After thousands of years, the eagle is getting pretty sick of this, and would quite like to retire to a quiet life terrorising mice, small rodents and Arnie the Griffin (as if!)

Favourite Foods: Anything but raw liver. No, really. Anything!

Likes: Soaring through the skies, thinking deep and meaningful thoughts, chasing clouds and Arnie the Griffin.

Dislikes: Liver, liver, liver (did I say liver?).

Dangers: An angry Caucasian Eagle can tear even a god to bits with its sharp claws and beak. Do not mention the words Prometheus, liver, or ask it if it's had a ripping day.

Demon's Top Tip: The Caucasian Eagle likes a beakful or two of very finely chopped spearmint and parsley mixed with its lunchtime ambrosia. Apparently it takes the taste of Titan liver away.

FLYING HORSES (PEGASI)

Description: Unlike their big horse cousin Pegasus (who is unique), the flying horses are only about the size of a large pony. Their coats are usually a deep onyx black, but there are occasional palominos, whites and chestnuts. They have two small stubby gold horns and their wings have golden edges to the feathers. They live in herds, obeying one boss horse, who can be either male or female. The boss

Nereids *(NEAR-ee-ids)*: Sea nymphs (girls) – their brothers are Nerites. Daughters of Nereus, the Old Man of the Sea.

Nereus *(NEH-re-us)*: The Old Man of the Sea, a shapeshifter fond of wrestling heroes like Heracles.

Nymphs *(NIMFS)*: Giggly, girly, dancing nature spirits.

Orion *(oh-RY-on)*: Starry hunter killed by a scorpion.

Orpheus *(or-FEE-us)*: Magnificent musician who tried to rescue his beloved Eurydice from the Underworld. (Massive fail there, then.)

Pandora *(pan-DOR-ah)*: The first human woman. Accidentally opened a jar full of evil.

Prometheus *(pruh-MEE-thee-us)*: Gave fire to mankind, and was sentenced to eternal torture by bird-pecking.

Satyrs *(SAY-ters)*: 50% goat, 50% human. 100% party animal.

Silenus *(sy-LEE-nus)*: Dionysus's best friend. Old and wise, but not that good at beast-care.

Tritons *(TRY-tuns)*: Half man, half two-tailed fish.

PLACES:

Aeolia *(ay-OH-lee-ah)*: Ancient name for Thessaly, an area of central Greece and bloody battle playground of Ares and Eris.

Arcadia *(ar-CAY-dee-a)*: Wooded hills in Greece where the nymphs and dryads like to play.

Macriss *(MACK-riss)*: Large seahorse-shaped island off the Greek coast where Poseidon has his second palace.

Mount Pelion *(PEE-lee-on)*: Mountain in Northern Greece and happy home of Chiron the centaur and his apprentices.

Tartarus *(TAR-ta-russ)*: A delightful torture dungeon miles below the Underworld.

The Underworld: Hades' happy little kingdom of dead people, also known as Hell in Northern parts.

Favourite Foods: Ambrosia cake, and plenty of it. Also apples.

Likes: Demon, Hera, carrying as many buckets and brooms as it can fit in its nine mouths, fluttering its long, curly eyelashes, drooling.

Dislikes: Heracles, swords, loud noises, garlic.

Dangers: When threatened, the Hydra's normally harmless drool turns to poisonous bile that melts flesh.

Demon's Top Tip: Keep your stocks of ambrosia cake safely locked away, or Doris will gobble the lot. You do NOT want a sick Hydra on your hands. Nine vomiting heads? Nuh-uh!

UNICORNS

Description: Adult unicorns are off-white, horse-like creatures with dark red heads, and a tri-coloured horn in the middle of their foreheads. Foals can range from dark to light grey. They have blue eyes and are very gentle. They produce a thick, creamy vanilla-scented milk, which the goddesses on Olympus like to use in their baths. Can only be milked by females. Their milk is also a good remedy for poisoning.

Favourite Foods: Ambrosia mixed with honey and vanilla, mist flavoured with lavender.

Likes: Being sung to or played to on a lyre, being stroked by young ladies, neighing at the full moon, galloping very fast.

Dislikes: Men, boys, gods.

Dangers: Can kick and bite. If you are male, beware of horn, which has a tip sharper than Ares's spear.

Demon's Top Tip: Unicorns are beautiful, but hard to get near if you're a boy, so bribe the nymphs to look after them, especially at milking time.

Have you discovered all of Demon's adventures?

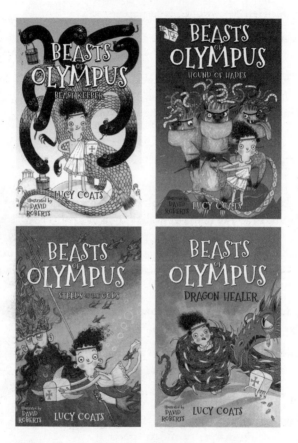

Available from all good bookshops and in ebook
Find out more at
www.piccadillypress.co.uk